The Not So Distant Future

By Raven Snow

Text Copyright © 2014 by Raven Snow
All Rights Reserved

No one would have believed in the last years of the nineteenth century that this world was being watched keenly and closely by intelligences greater than man's and yet as mortal as his own; that as men busied themselves about their various concerns they were scrutinized and studied, perhaps almost as narrowly as a man with a microscope might scrutinize the transient creatures that swarm and multiply in a drop of water....Yet across the gulf of space, minds that are to our minds as ours are to those of the beasts that perish, intellects vast and cool and unsympathetic, regarded this earth with envious eyes, and slowly and surely drew their plans against us...
H.G. Wells, "The War of the Worlds"
1898

The thrust into outer space of the satellite, spheres and missiles marked the beginning of another epoch in the long story of mankind - the chapter of the space age. In the five or more billions of years the scientists tell us it has taken to form the earth, in the three or more billion years of development of the human race, there has never been a greater, a more abrupt or staggering evolution. We deal now not with things of this world alone, but with the illimitable distances and as yet unfathomed mysteries of the universe....
And through all this welter of change and development your mission remains fixed, determined, inviolable. It is to win our wars. The soldier above all other people prays for peace, for he must suffer and bear the deepest wounds and scars of war.
General Douglas MacArthur's Farewell Speech to the Cadets at West Point
1962

4 July

It was too bright in the room.

That was the first thing I thought when I opened my eyes.

Still blinking away sleep, I sat up. Across from my bunk, there was a window. Crisp, white sunshine spilled through it onto the floor, like an overturned glass of chardonnay; the sky I could see above Scarcliff's quad, three floors below, was a perfect, pale panel of blue. It was stiflingly hot in the room. Though I had crawled into bed the night before in just a pair of boxers, my back and chest were sticky with sweat. Clearly, the dorm's air conditioning wasn't working.

Nor was my alarm clock. I picked it up off my nightstand and frowned at its blank digital face. Okay, I remember thinking, so, the power was out. Why the hell would the power be out on a beautiful, sunny summer day?

And where the hell was Sergeant Donovan?

My dorm room at Scarcliff was small, and spartan. Kicking the covers off, I crossed it, threw open the door. There was just one window out in the dark-paneled hallway, down at the far end by the communal bathroom. Apparently even the emergency lights were out, which I had never known to happen before, because the hallway was very dim. Shadows drifted across it like smoke.

I listened hard, half-expecting to hear Donovan storming up the stairs to demand an explanation for why the flag had not been raised at dawn, as per protocol - but the only sound in the entire dorm seemed to be coming from the one door standing ajar, three rooms down from mine.

Squaring my shoulders - which brought me up to about five-foot-seven, not exactly an imposing height - I marched down the hall, barefoot and boxer-clad, and tapped on the doorframe.

"Enter," a voice called out.

My school, Scarcliff Military Academy, was a venerated Southern institution. The dormitory looked the part: hardwood floors, blown-glass light fixtures, antique wainscoting. The furnishings, however, were simple: a bunk bed, a bureau, a study desk, and a nightstand for every cadet. This room's occupant had added some personal touches. Stacks of old milk crates holding books and CDs. Movie posters and concert flyers papered over the walls. Tacked to the ceiling, like a giant middle finger in the face of our commanding officers, a tie-dyed peace sign tapestry.

Said occupant was seated cross-legged on his bunk, one finger marking his spot in a dog-eared copy of *Siddhartha*. Kyle Brody looked up at me, and smirked. "Morning, Lieutenant," he drawled.

I rolled my eyes. Brody did not take the chain of command at Scarcliff seriously - which was why, after three years as classmates, I was a Cadet First Lieutenant, Brody still a lowly Cadet Private. He had actually been promoted to Corporal at the end of our ninth grade year, but a nasty incident with cherry bombs in the public restroom had gotten him busted back down to Private. If his father hadn't been who he was, he probably would have been kicked out.

"What's going on?" I demanded.

It came out accusingly. Like I thought Brody (nobody called him Kyle) was responsible for shutting off the power to the dorm. Brody shrugged. He, too, was in boxers, his window cracked to tempt a nonexistent breeze. "Beats me. I woke up an hour ago and realized the electricity was out."

"Did you raise the flag?" I asked.

"That's your job, isn't it, Lieutenant?"

Brody's smirk had deepened. I flushed. This was classic Brody. He could have woken me up, once he realized the lights were out; but he wouldn't have, first of all because Kyle Brody hated taking orders from anyone, especially other cadets, and most especially *me*, and second of all because he would have known it would reflect poorly on my spotless record to sleep through flag duty on the Fourth of July, of all days. "Have you seen Sergeant Donovan?" I asked.

"Nope." Brody was supremely unconcerned. "I figure he's still down in his quarters, sleeping off that fifth of Jack Daniels he snuck off to buy last night."

I bit my tongue, wanting to say something in Donovan's defense; but I, too, had seen the headlights of Donovan's pickup scrape by my window just after lights-out the previous night. The sergeant's drinking problem was common knowledge among the cadets.

Nevertheless, Donovan was one of my favorite instructors - not to mention that, with Colonel Thorne and the other instructors away for the holiday break, he was Scarcliff's officer-in-charge. "Get dressed," I commanded, pushing off the doorframe. "Meet me in the hall in five minutes. We'll go wake him up together."

Brody sighed. "River - "

"I said *now*, Private."

There was enough bark to my voice, although I was shorter, skinnier, and all around less cool than Kyle Brody, to cause him to raise his hands in surrender. Pretending he would not flip me off the moment my back was turned, I marched smartly out of the room.

6

****

Five minutes later, we were picking our way down the stairs from the third floor.

The dorm's stairwells were enclosed, with only a strip of narrow windows running along the ceiling to allow in any light. I held onto the banister. The darkness felt like a living tissue around me, currents of air snatching at my skin like invisible hands. By the time we reached the bottom, my tee-shirt was damp with sweat along the spine.

I told myself it was just the humidity.

It was brighter on the first floor. Together, Brody and I crossed the common area with its couches, study tables, and floor-to-ceiling windows to the officers' quarters on the other side. Tentatively, I knocked on the door with SERGEANT BEAU DONOVAN, ARMY INSTRUCTOR emblazoned on the brass nameplate.

No one answered.

Brody slouched against the wall, looking bored. Like me, he was half in uniform now - camouflage trousers and white tee-shirt. It was too hot inside the dorm for fatigue jackets. I had laced on my boots. Brody was barefoot. He ran a hand through his close-cropped blonde hair, which wasn't quite close-cropped enough to be regulation, studying me from under his lashes. "What now, Lieutenant? You want to organize a search party? We might be a little low on volunteers, seeing as it's just you and me left on campus..."

As if I might have forgotten that.

I had pretended not to care yesterday while the other cadets were piling into airport taxis and family vans, headed off to spend the holiday weekend, and our two-week break between terms, with their respective families. I had planned to spend my two weeks at Scarcliff, like usual, getting a head start on next term's reading list, filling out college applications, and practicing my skills down at the rifle range. I had not planned on spending any more time around Kyle Brody than was absolutely necessary. "We should check the commissary," I said, as it was becoming obvious Donovan was not inside the dorm. "He might be over there, talking to the kitchen staff or something."

Brody nodded and slid the slender black case he had been toying with - probably a contraband cell phone - back in his pocket. "Sounds good to me. I'm starving."

Outside, swampy Virginia heat hit us like a wall. Shading my eyes against a hazy midmorning sun, I scanned the dark windows of the brick classroom buildings; the tops of the budding trees that lined the central quad; the unused guardhouse by the wrought-iron gate that cordoned Scarcliff off from the main road. I had never appreciated until just then how isolated Scarcliff really was. Normally, campus was bustling, home to twenty-five hundred cadets. I had expected it to be quieter this morning with everyone gone for break, but this silence was oppressive. It took me a moment to realize why.

No birds were singing.

The commissary was a one-story building sandwiched between the library and the fitness center. It was left unlocked twenty-four seven, though meals were served only three times a day; there were vending machines in the vestibule, and an old ping pong table that saw a lot of use. When you weren't allowed TVs in your room, cell phones were banned for cadets, and the only Internet connection was on the computers in the library, there wasn't much to do besides read, workout, or play ping pong with your buddies. Brody gave the net an affectionate flick as we walked past, our footsteps echoing on the hardwood.

Just inside the doors to the dining area, I stopped, looking around. The place was deserted. Shadows had gathered thickly around the long, empty wooden benches, behind the steam tables that fronted the dark, silent kitchen. A tightness had begun to form in my chest.

"Guess we missed chow," Brody said, lightly - but when I glanced at him, I noticed that he was looking around as well, forehead slightly furrowed. Because Brody wasn't stupid, I was sure he was thinking the same thing I was. We hadn't missed breakfast. No one had ever been here to fix it.

I had been staying at Scarcliff over breaks for three years, since ninth grade. In all of that time, the kitchen staff had never just not shown up to fix a meal.

And again: Where the hell was Donovan?

Brody turned and walked back to the vestibule. I hurried after him, letting the wooden doors to the dining area swing shut. "Maybe we should call someone," I said, and instantly wished I had issued it as an order instead, the way my father would have: *We're going to call someone.*

"How are we going to do that?" Brody stopped before the vending machines, critically eyeing the candy and sodas on display. "We don't have cell phones, remember?" I thought of the black case I had just seen him put in his pocket, but it didn't seem worth the fight to challenge him on it. I thought, at the time, he would be worried about me confiscating it. As I most likely would have. Rules were rules, even if you thought they were stupid. "The only landline I know of is in Colonel Thorne's office. Now, if you're suggesting we break in..."

He grinned, wickedly. That put the possibility right out of my mind. Anything Brody thought sounded like a good idea probably wasn't. Who were we going to call, anyway? The police? There was no emergency. Brody and I were teenagers; we could handle being on our own during a power outage. Our parents? Even if I had been sure my father would answer his phone when I called, there was no chance Sergeant Donovan wouldn't lose his job if it got back to Colonel Thorne that he had left the cadets in his charge unattended on campus. And what would I say if I spoke to my father, anyway? It wasn't like one of us was bleeding to death. There was no immediate danger. The lights would probably be back on any second -

"What are you doing?" I burst out.

"What's it look like I'm doing?" Brody spoke evenly. He was reaching around the snack machine, unplugging it from the wall. As I watched, he began to tip it forward, the muscles in his arms straining. "Vending machines don't work without electricity, Lieutenant. I don't know about you, but I'm starv- "

"Stop it." I yanked Brody away from the machine before he could tip it over. It rocked back into place, the coins in the bottom clanging as it settled into position.

Brody jerked away from me, exasperated. "Jesus Christ, River, what's your problem? We have to eat, man. If Donovan expects us to go hungry until he decides to turn his drunk ass up, he can - "

"First of all," I interrupted, patiently, "we both ate dinner last night. I doubt you're in danger of starving to death in less than twenty-four hours." Brody scowled. "Secondly, we don't need to break into a vending machine to get food. Right through those doors," I pointed, "there is a kitchen equipped to feed several hundred teenage boys. If we go and look, I have a feeling we'll find something edible lying around."

Brody looked sheepish. "Good point," he said.

I smirked.

The kitchen was massive, and a bit spooky with no lights on, no windows to let in the sun. I wished I had brought along a flashlight - I kept one in my nightstand, just in case - but it wasn't so dark we couldn't see what we were doing. More importantly, I refused to admit to Brody that I found the way the shadows pooled on the stainless steel surfaces creepy. In the walk-in pantry, we found shelves of canned fruit, some loaves of bread, and rows and rows of industrial-sized peanut butter jars. Brody ducked into one of the walk-in freezers and emerged with a tub of chocolate chip ice cream.

I raised an eyebrow. "Ice cream for breakfast?"

"Why not?" Brody shrugged. His answer for everything, I thought.

We carried the food back to the vestibule, spread it on the floor and ate with our backs against the wall. With the main doors propped open, it was almost pleasant inside the commissary. Like an indoor picnic. Brody poked a straw down inside his carton of milk. "How come you didn't go home for break?" he asked.

I took the time to swallow a mouthful of peanut butter before answering. "I don't know. My dad doesn't get a lot of downtime. If I was just going to spend the whole two weeks by myself anyway, I thought I might as well stay here, get some work done."

"What about hanging with your friends back home?"

For a second, I had been afraid Brody was about to ask about my mother. As this was the first actual conversation we had ever had, it wasn't like we knew much about each other's lives. All I really knew about Brody was that he was good-looking, well-to-do, and popular. Basically everything I was not. "D.C. isn't really home for me," I explained. "My father wasn't stationed at the Pentagon until just before I started here at Scarcliff. I never even knew anyone my own age there."

"Where'd you live before that?"

"All over. Germany. Texas. Italy. Hawaii. Wherever my father got transferred, basically."

"So you're a real army brat, huh?" Brody grinned, swiping a smear of ice cream off his chin. He had stretched his legs out full length in front of him, toward the ping pong table. A gust of wind blew the lightweight plastic ball onto the floor. It rolled into one of the vestibule's shadowy corners. I watched it. I wasn't hungry anymore, all of a sudden. I kept listening, hoping to hear Donovan calling out to us, or the hum of appliances as the power came back on.

"What about you?" I asked, as Brody dug out another spoonful of ice cream. "Don't you usually go home to Boston over breaks?"

"I usually go to somebody *else's* home over breaks," Brody corrected, cheerfully. "Anywhere I don't have to put up with my old man telling me what a disappointment I am, and my mom complaining about me being a 'bad influence' on the little kids."

10

"You have brothers and sisters?" I was instantly intrigued. As an only child, I found the idea of siblings fascinating. I drew my knees up under my chin. "How many of each?"

"Three," Brody said. "All brothers."

"Are they younger, or older?"

"Younger. The youngest is just starting kindergarten next month."

"Don't you miss them, being gone so much of the year?"

"I guess. I don't know them that well." Brody had begun licking his spoon clean. "My parents packed me off to boarding school when I was nine, right after my dad won his first big election. This is the third school I've been to. The only one I haven't been expelled from, so far."

Not for lack of trying, I thought. "Why did they - "

"Shh!" Brody sat bolt upright suddenly, knocking over his carton of milk. A small white stream trickled out onto the hardwood. I made an involuntary sound of protest, but Brody shushed me. "Did you hear that?" he said.

"Hear what?" My heart was thudding. I cast around, seeing only shadows - gathered thickest in the corners, like hunched-over old men, pressed like faces up against the glass in the dining room doors. I glanced at Brody. If he was just messing with me -

"I heard something," Brody insisted, like he knew what I was thinking. He jumped up, eyes on the square of sunlight spilling through the commissary doors. "I think somebody's out there."

He jerked his chin toward the quad. I looked. All I could see was sunshine, green grass waving in the breeze around the still-bare flag pole. "It's probably Sergeant Donovan," I said, and before Brody could stop me - though why he would have, I wasn't sure - I hurried through the open doors.

I had not taken a step beyond them when I heard it, too.

After the dimness inside, the sunlight was blinding. Shading my eyes with one hand, I turned, toward the paved drive that wound up from the academy's wrought-iron gate. My mouth tasted of ashes.

I shouted for Brody. Then I started running.

The man stumbling up the drive kept his feet until I was almost even with him. Then his legs seemed to go out, both at the same time; he crumpled straight to the concrete, and I fell to my knees beside him. My pulse was jumping in my fingertips and toes. "Sergeant?" I said, softly.

The sound of the gate squawking as the wind caught it nearly drowned out the word. Some part of me realized that must have been what Brody had heard - the gate squawking on its metal hinges as

Sergeant Donovan had pushed it open. The rest of me, however, was busy trying to recall everything I had ever learned in Advanced Field Medicine about treating gunshot wounds.

That had to be what had ripped open Donovan's stomach. The front of his fatigue jacket was soaked in blood; when I pulled the cloth aside, I almost gagged at the two huge, bloody holes punched through his abdomen. Meaty scraps of tissue straggled out of them. A loop of something red and slimy was visible inside the lowest one. I heard someone behind me suck in a breath, and looked up to see Brody standing over me, backlit by the sun. The tips of his spiky blonde hair looked like they were on fire.

"What the fuck?" he whispered.

"We have to call 911," I said. My hands were shaking, yet I managed to tear the tee-shirt off over my head. I pressed it down on Donovan's wounds. Donovan moaned. He was making gurgling noises in the back of his throat. They might have been attempts at words, but I could not make them out. "Your cell phone - "

"I don't have a cell phone," Brody said.

Right at that moment, I believed him. "Okay, then check his pockets," I said. "See if he has one."

To Brody's credit, he did not hesitate: He dropped to his knees and reached carefully into the pockets of Donovan's trousers, front and back. I picked up one of the sergeant's hands. I wasn't really thinking about it. Donovan's face was a funny shade of greenish-white. There were flecks of pink on his lips, from the blood and spit frothing over his chin. "Well?" I said, thinly.

Brody shook his head. He was very pale. "He doesn't have one."

"Then we'll have to use a landline." The evenness of my voice astounded me. "The colonel's office - "

"I'm on it."

Just like that, Brody jumped up, and flashed off across the quad. "Bring back a first-aid kit!" I shouted after him.

Donovan gurgled again. I looked down. Donovan had hazel eyes. They were only half-open, but his stare, I would never forget, was fixed on my face. Beau Donovan was a strapping man. Seeing him in uniform, striding around campus with his graying hair still worn in a buzz-cut, it wasn't hard to imagine him storming into battle. Now, somehow, he looked shrunken, his eyes drawn too far back inside his skull. I tried to quiet him, but he gathered a rattling breath in his throat and forced out two words.

Fort Green.

"What?" I said. For some reason, whispering.

Donovan licked his lips - and began coughing. His fingers, sticky with blood, slid out of mine. Never had I seen someone's face contort with such agony. I made some meaningless sound of comfort, pressed my hands down harder on Donovan's wounds, doing my utmost to staunch the bleeding. My tee-shirt was soaked right through. Where the hell was Brody - ?

At that exact instant Brody reappeared, dropping down on the asphalt across from me. He was clutching a white first-aid kit against his chest. "Are they coming?" I asked, desperately, ears already pricked for sirens. But Brody shook his head. His eyes were huge, and darkly blue.

"I couldn't call out," he said. "The phones are down. The line's just - dead."

I stared at him. None of this made any sense. The electricity going out was one thing. But now the phones as well? And Donovan? Who the hell had done this to Donovan? "We'll have to drive him to the hospital, then," I said, sounding a thousand times calmer than I felt. "He must have his truck keys on him. See if you can - "

"He's dead."

Brody said it so simply, it took a second for the words to sink in.

Up until then, I had only ever seen one dead body in my life, and my mother had not looked like Sergeant Donovan at the moment of her death. *She* had been wrapped in her favorite quilt, surrounded by nurses and machines in the bedroom that had become more like a hospital room during her short, sudden illness. I remember thinking she had looked like she was sleeping and might wake at any moment when my father squeezed my shoulder and told me it was over, she was gone.

Beau Donovan did not appear to be sleeping. A thin puddle of bloody saliva had pooled under his jaw; his head had fallen to one side, against the concrete. His eyes were still half-open, a sliver of white visible below the lids. His hands had frozen into fists against his sides. Like he had died trying to hold onto life.

I stood up. In that moment, I could hear everything, feel everything - the wind sighing in the trees that marched right up to the edge of campus; the sun warming the back of my head, my bare shoulders and spine. I could smell Virginia clay beneath the grass, and the rust-salt scent of Donovan's blood, and the stale, sharp odor of my own sweat, and Brody's. When Brody reached out, flicking a fly away from Donovan's lips,

I saw, as if for the first time, the freckles on the backs of his hands, the bones that connected his fingers to his wrists.

I looked down at my own hands. They were covered in blood up to the wrists.

"What?" I said. Aware, suddenly, that Brody was talking to me.

"I said," Brody rose, still holding the goddamn first-aid kit; his expression was grim, "I think it's time we got the hell out of here, Lieutenant."

Later, I would not remember returning to the dorm, stripping off my bloodstained trousers, or standing under the shower spray in the dark. When I came back to myself, as if waking from some strange dream, I was sitting on my bunk bed in a clean pair of boxers and a fresh white tee-shirt, staring at the picture of my mother on my nightstand.

It had been snapped on a beach somewhere. Hawaii, perhaps. My father had tried to throw it out with the rest of Mom's belongings, but I had swiped the picture on the sly - hidden it in the back of my sock drawer until my father, General Augustus Lane, had packed me off to Scarcliff less than six months later.

In the photograph, my mother was holding onto a wide-brimmed straw hat the ocean breeze was trying to snatch away. She was laughing. Though a pair of oversized sunglasses hid her eyes, I knew they would have been dancing, as well. My eyes were the only physical feature of hers I had inherited. They were gray-green, like the ocean before a storm. The rest of my features - my dark hair, my compact frame - all came directly from my father. Except what was ruggedly handsome on him, on me somehow didn't quite fit together. Like I had been assembled just slightly off-center. No one would ever have called me handsome, though people did often comment on my eyes.

Were those really the thoughts running through my mind as I sat there in my dorm room, with crescents of Sergeant Donovan's blood still crusted under my fingernails? I would never be certain, looking back. The next thing I really remember was hearing a footstep. Looking up, I watched Brody's broad shoulders fill my doorway.

He was still pale. He had donned a boonie cap, slung a standard issue army-green rucksack over his arm. I rose quickly, went to my closet and retrieved a clean pair of trousers. Brody leaned against my doorframe. "I found Donovan's keys," he announced, quietly.

"Did you see his truck around anywhere?" I asked. Brody shook his head.

We would have to walk, then. Into town, to the sheriff's station. We had left Sergeant Donovan's body on the quad, covered over with a tarp Brody had found in the maintenance shed; I had still been thinking clearly enough at that point to know you didn't move a dead body when the person had died under suspicious circumstances. The sheriff would have to investigate.

It was a ten-mile hike from Scarcliff Academy into Peach Tree, the nearest town. Fortunately, we had plenty of daylight left. And once we hit the main road, I reasoned, a passerby was likely to pick us up...

"You okay?"

I blinked. Realizing I was standing motionless in front of my closet, staring into the dust motes dancing in a sunbeam - the power had yet to come back on - I turned around. "Did you get some bottles of water from the commissary, like I told you to?"

Brody patted his rucksack. "Yessir. It's all in here. More than enough to get us into town." He paused. "Did...Did Donovan say anything to you, while I was gone? About who...who did that to him?"

I shook my head. "All he said was, 'Fort Green.'"

Although I was tucking the flashlight from my nightstand into the side pocket of my trousers when I said it, from the corner of my eye, I saw Brody stand up straight. "Fort Green?" he echoed.

"Yeah. It's an army base. About fifty miles northeast of here, up the Interstate toward Charlottesville."

"I know what Fort Green is." Brody sounded irritated. "I was just thinking that I saw it on the news last night, before lights-out. The president was there, giving some big speech to the troops for Independence Day."

We looked at one another.

I looked away first. There was no reason to panic, I told myself. Donovan had been in shock from pain and blood loss, barely conscious when he had uttered those words. For all I knew, Fort Green was somewhere he had been stationed. He could have had friends or family there. I sat down to lace up my boots. "What do you think did that to him?"

"It had to be a large caliber weapon," Brody said. I raised my eyes. Since when did Kyle Brody know anything about weapons? This was the guy who had refused to take Military History on the grounds that all war was immoral and inhumane. "You saw his wounds. If he had been shot at close range, there would have been burns around them, from the muzzle flash. It must have been a high-powered rifle, fired from a distance, to make wounds like that."

I didn't think the wounds looked like they had been made by any bullets I had ever seen. Granted, at that time I hadn't seen many gunshot wounds. "Wouldn't we have heard something like that?" I said. Mostly thinking out loud.

"I think - I think maybe I did." Still hovering in my doorway, Brody shifted his weight. "Something woke me up this morning. A - sound. I lay there for a minute, waiting to see if I would hear it again - "

"You lay there listening for more *gunshots*?"

I was incredulous. Brody flushed. "I didn't think it was gunshots, all right? It's the Fourth of July. I thought some redneck just got a little gung-ho with setting off his fireworks."

"Newsflash, Private: People don't set off fireworks until it's *dark*. You can't see them in the daylight." I stood up. The shock of Donovan's death was wearing off; the gears in my mind were grinding together again. Colonel Thorne liked to tell me I had "command potential," or what my father called the ability to keep your shit together under pressure. "Where did these 'sounds' come from?"

"I don't know, man." Brody's tone was exasperated. "I told you, they woke me up. Then I didn't hear them anymore. I'm sorry I didn't go out and do recon - "

Or at least wake me up, in which case Sergeant Donovan might still be alive, because we could have gone out looking for him... "Think, Brody," I insisted, with as much patience as I could manage. "You were lying in bed. Your room faces east. How far away were the sounds you heard? A mile? Two miles? Were they on-campus? Off-campus? In the woods? Back toward town?"

"Jesus Christ, River, what does it *matter*?"

"It matters," I said, "because for all we know, whoever shot Donovan is still out there. And since we're about to go hiking down the main highway, I'd like some idea of whether or not we're walking straight into an ambush."

"I told you," Brody said. "I found Donovan's keys."

He held them up - a collection of silver keys on a GO ARMY keychain. "Without Donovan's truck -," I started.

"I'm not talking about his truck," Brody said. "There's a key to his room on here, as well. You know he keeps a rifle in there. His old M16, from his combat glory days."

For a full ten seconds, I just stared at him. Then I said: "What?"

"Donovan's army rifle." Brody spoke slowly, like he thought my brains had been addled by something. "You and I both know he has one. You're on the varsity rifle team. I've seen Donovan tote his old M16 down to the shooting range to show off when you guys are practicing. You said it yourself. Whoever did that to Donovan - " neither of us seemed able to use the word "murdered" " - might still be around. Here we are, no phone, no car, no way to call for help. I don't know about you, but I'm not setting off into town without some way to defend myself."

"No." Tabling for the moment the question of whether or not Brody could even fire a weapon - true to form, he had always refused to take part at the shooting range - I shook my head. "Neither one of us has a permit to carry a firearm, on or off school grounds. How do you think the sheriff will take it if two juveniles walk into his town toting a military assault rifle?"

"Do you think I actually give a shit about that?"

Probably not, I allowed, but, "I do," I said. "And since I outrank you, Private, it doesn't really matter what you do or don't give a shit about."

Brody laughed. He actually laughed, though there wasn't any humor in it. "I've got a newsflash for you, *sir*," he said, nastily. "We aren't in the army. We're in fucking *high school*, and somebody just blew the fucking guts out of one of our fucking teachers. So if you want to try court martialing me," Brody said, "you go right ahead. Because as of now, I am done with this wannabe Medal of Honor bullshit you're so caught up in. *Lieutenant*."

Amazingly, I felt a sting of embarrassment spread across my cheeks. It was stupid - ridiculous beyond belief - that I could still care what Kyle Brody thought of me. Not that Brody had ever made any secret about that, from the moment we had met in ninth grade. All of those times he had saluted as I walked by in the commissary, then cracked up with his buddies before I was even out of earshot. The eyerolls and snickers when I answered a question in class, or lined the cadets in my company up on the quad for weekly inspection. Brody treated Scarcliff like a joke. Anybody who bought into it was, to him, worse than an idiot. Barely worth being looked down upon.

But we had bigger problems at the moment. We needed to find the sheriff, bring back the cavalry before whoever had killed Donovan escaped - or worse, attacked somebody else. A killer was on the loose. Soldier or not, I had a duty to report that.

Without another word to Brody, I marched out into the hall. I didn't bother to see if he was following.

*****

Sergeant Donovan's room was as neat as I had expected. The double bed was made up with olive-green sheets. A handful of loose change shared the desk in the corner with a battered laptop and a new-ish copy of *Newsweek*. There were no family photographs, but there were several pictures of Donovan in desert camouflage, posed with guys from his army unit, lined up in cheap plastic frames along the windowsill.

The rifle was in his foot locker - which wasn't even locked. Underneath it, I found a Beretta. What would Colonel Thorne have said, had he known Donovan kept a loaded pistol at the foot of his bed, buried beneath a spare blanket and a moth-eaten poncho?

Would it have saved Donovan's life, if he had taken the pistol with him last night?

The only thing that made sense to me was that Donovan must never have returned to campus after driving off. His bed did not appear slept in. What had happened in the twelve hours between him leaving campus and him stumbling through the gate that morning was a mystery I was not, at the time, equipped to solve.

When I turned, Brody was standing in the hallway. Like he thought it would be bad luck to cross the threshold of a dead man's room. I slung the rifle over my shoulder by its strap. "Have you ever fired a gun before?" I asked.

Brody rolled his eyes. "Are we seriously about to have a macho pissing contest right now, Lieutenant?"

"I'm seriously not giving you a weapon if you don't know how to use it," I replied. "You'll just end up shooting yourself with it. Or me. Maybe even on accident."

Brody's lips twitched at that. "I can shoot," he said, calmly.

I was not certain I believed him, but I handed over a handful of extra magazines and the Beretta, butt-first, anyway. "And stop calling me 'lieutenant,'" I said, still holding onto the pistol, "unless you plan on taking orders from me again."

Smirking a little, Brody nodded.

The common area seemed brighter than I remembered - probably because the sun was higher in the sky; it had to be nearly noon. Brody, busy stowing the extra ammo in his rucksack, bumped into me from behind on the front steps. "What the - "

"Where is he?" I said.

I all but whispered it. The moisture had dried up in my mouth like I had swallowed a cupful of acid.

The tarp we had placed so carefully over Donovan's body was still on the quad, weighted down on the corners with rocks. I had placed those rocks there myself, afraid the wind would blow the tarp away otherwise. There was nothing underneath it now. No body. Nothing but a swath of blood-soaked grass.

The unnatural silence filled up my ears like cotton. I looked - at the still-open doors of the commissary; the half-open gate down the drive; the splintered door of the administration building, kicked in by Brody when he had been desperately seeking a landline to call the paramedics. Shadows drifted across the classroom buildings' upper stories. As though hiding whoever - or whatever - was standing on the other side of those blank, black windowpanes, staring down at us.

A shiver started in my shoulders, worked its way down my spine.

"I don't believe this," Brody said. He was holding the pistol loosely at his side, scanning the buildings around the quad just like I was. "Man, he was *dead*. He couldn't just - get up and walk away..."

Someone had to take him, I knew both of us were thinking. Someone who was probably still close by. Watching us.

In my bones, I could *feel* them watching us.

"Come on," I said.

The walk from the dormitory to the main gate was the longest I had ever taken in my life. There was no cover - no trees, no buildings to crouch behind; the gate centered a ten-foot-tall brick privacy fence that stretched halfway around the campus. Behind the dorms was only forest, acres and acres of forest; going out the back door would have been no help to us, because, without the highway to follow, I had no idea how to find the nearest town, nor any map to lead us there - nor any GPS-equipped cell phone. The only option we had was to walk as quickly as we could without actually running to the main road.

The gate was blowing gently in the breeze, rusted hinges squawking softly. Every time one of my boots scraped the asphalt, I expected to hear an ear-shattering blast, feel a sniper's bullet pierce my spine. I held the rifle tight against my side, ready to swing it up at any moment -

But we slipped through the gate without seeing or hearing anything. Without any discussion about it, we let ourselves break into a run.

The road was a narrow, paved strip for less than a mile out to the highway. Cottonwoods and aspens to our left and right provided shade and shadows. The shade was welcome. The shadows I could have done without. The wind picked up again, whispering in the leaves above our heads; there were still no birds calling, no squirrels chattering, no animals rustling in the undergrowth. The power lines overhead were silent, void of their usual electric hum - a sound so constant I had never been aware of it, until it was gone. My footfalls seemed too loud in my own ears. I almost yelped when Brody grabbed my arm, jerking me to a stop.

"Look," he said, holding his side as he tried to catch his breath.

I looked - to where a Superman-red Ford pickup with rust over the wheel wells was parked, right in the middle of the left-hand lane. Brody shifted the rucksack higher on his shoulders, pistol still in hand. The twin Vs of sweat on his tee-shirt, front and back, matched the ones on my own; the day, despite the breeze, was broiling. "Is that...?"

"It's Donovan's," I said. I had seen the sergeant's pickup in the faculty lot nearly every day for three years now. Sometimes, I thought the reason Donovan and I got on so well was that Scarcliff was the only real home either of us had.

The pickup's windows were rolled down. Brody opened the door (it was unlocked) and slid the pilfered key into the ignition. He turned it.

Nothing happened. *Nothing.* The starter didn't sputter. The engine didn't cough. "It's dead," Brody announced, unnecessarily.

I shivered. *He's dead,* Brody had said, back on the quad. I looked around. Brush grew thick up against the trees here; to either side of the road, deep, muddy ditches were half-filled with rainwater. If Donovan's truck had stalled out here, less than three miles from campus, there would have been no reason for him not to stay on the main road to walk back. But a sniper could easily have hidden in any of these trees, especially after dark - although, I reminded myself, if what Brody had heard that morning had been gunshots, Donovan had not met his fate until two hours after sunrise.

The real questions were: What had Donovan still been doing out here after sunrise? And why would anybody want to shoot Sergeant Donovan?

Brody had walked around behind the truck, inspecting it for damage. I propped my rifle against the running board and leaned across the cab - only to leap back with a curse: The truck had rocked sideways. I whirled around, to see Brody, pushing against the back of the truck from the passenger's side with both hands. I glared at him. My heart was thudding against my ribs. "What the fuck, man?"

"I was seeing whether it was out of gas," Brody said, innocently. "It isn't. I can hear sloshing in the tank." He took his boonie hat off; wiped sweat off his brow with his forearm; and turned to squint down the highway. It was empty, as far as the eye could see. At noon on a perfect summer day.

I picked up the small, shiny silver box I had been reaching for inside the truck. It was Donovan's cell phone. I punched the power button.

Somehow, I was not surprised when it did not turn on.

"No dice?" Brody guessed, looking at me across the truck bed. I shook my head. That tightness was back in my chest again, squeezing a sour taste up into my throat. The interior of Donovan's pickup smelled like him - like Marlboro cigarettes and Old Spice cologne. A bottle of Jack Daniels, unopened, occupied the passenger's seat. It was still wrapped in a brown paper bag.

I closed the truck door as quietly as possible. The sound was still loud in the silence. "Looks like we're walking," I said.

"I'm thinking EMP," Brody said.

We were walking side-by-side down the highway, the center line separating us. Sunlight baked off the asphalt in waves. We had walked almost six miles now, without encountering a single car, truck, or semi - or another pedestrian. I kicked a rock out of my path. "What are you talking about?"

"A terrorist attack," Brody said. "Don't tell me you're not thinking it. Somebody sets off an electromagnetic pulse in the atmosphere, and it fries everything electronic. Cars. Lights. Cell phones." He nodded, indicating the cell phone I had, out of an abundance of optimism, tucked into the pocket of my trousers. Like it might spontaneously start working again.

Optimistic was not how I was feeling at the moment. I was hot, I was sweaty, the top of my head was being slow-broiled by the noonday sun, and my feet felt like superheated blocks of lead squeezed into heavy black combat boots. Brody didn't look much better. Sweat was trickling down his cheeks from under the brim of his hat. I could imagine how his shoulders must have been aching from toting that rucksack.

"Do you want me to carry that?" I offered.

"I got it," Brody said. I shrugged. *Suit yourself.* Brody always had to play the tough guy. Had it been possible for him to overcome that giant ego of his, he might have realized the nicest thing about being a soldier was not having to go everything alone. You always had your brothers - and your sisters - at your back. "Well? So what do you think?"

"About the EMP?" I said.

He shot me a look of thinly-veiled impatience. "Yes, Lieu- River. About the EMP."

"I think that sort of thing only happens in science fiction movies and spy thrillers," I said. "And I think it's a little soon to be jumping to conclusions about terrorist attacks. We've found one stalled car, one dead cell phone. That's not exactly the apocalypse."

"And Sergeant Donovan?"

"We don't know what happened to Donovan." I swallowed as I said it, glancing back down the road behind us. Sunlight shimmering off the concrete made it seem like I was looking through a force-field. Another gust of wind sighed among the cottonwoods; the shadows the sun had beaten back beyond the ditches stretched their spindly arms back out onto the road. The feeling of being watched had lessened as Scarcliff dropped further and further behind us, yet I kept imagining I was going to look back and see Sergeant Donovan standing in the distance, mouth frozen in a rictus grin.

"Hey," Brody said, suddenly.

I ground my teeth together. Could he *stop* doing that? "What?" I said.

"That looks like a building up there. Like a gas station or something." Brody pointed. I could see it now as well, through a break in trees up ahead: a small structure with a red tin roof, surrounded by a sea of asphalt. I swung the rifle down from my shoulder, double-checking that the safety was off.

"Let's check it out," I said, as lightly as I could manage. Brody nodded.

We left the road. Well, I left the road, and Brody followed me, like he thought I knew what I was doing. We picked our way across the deep ditch, climbed through the tangled undergrowth on the other side. It was cooler under the trees, cooler than I thought it should have been, even in the shade. Sunlight spearing through the canopy created puddles of golden light on the forest floor. Everything smelled damp and mossy.

I placed my feet carefully, trying not to snap broken twigs with my boots. Brody mirrored me. He had a white-knuckled grip on the Beretta. "Don't start shooting anything that moves, all right?" I said, impatiently.

"I'm not going to shoot anything, unless I have to," Brody fired back. Like of the two of us, I was the one more likely to go on a murderous rampage. I rolled my eyes. Brody had no idea what it meant to be a soldier, if he thought killing was all that it was. Creeping the last few feet forward, I crouched down in the tree line.

I'll admit it: I was starting to feel ridiculous. What were we doing, sneaking up on a gas station like it was an enemy camp? These weren't the jungles of Vietnam. This was rural Virginia, for Christ's sake. The most dangerous things around here were rednecks and raccoons. *And whatever killed Sergeant Donovan,* I thought. "Come on," I said, almost irritably, and led Brody out of the bushes.

The gas station appeared deserted. No lights in the windows. No cars in the lot. Of course, with the power off, they probably couldn't be open, I realized; no way to operate automated gas pumps without electricity. And they might have been closed anyway, for the July Fourth holiday. Except the sign in the front window was flipped to *open*. I tried the door handle. It was locked.

"Maybe they forgot to turn the sign around last night," I said.

"Maybe," Brody said. *Keep telling yourself that,* his tone implied.

Cupping my hands against the glass, I peered inside. With no lights on, I could only discern shapes that looked like racks of sunglasses, shelves of candy and chips, some freezer cases in the back - the gas station seemed to double as a convenience store. There was an ATM by the cash register -

Something moved, at the corner of my vision.

I gasped. It took me a moment to realize it was only Brody. Rather, it was Brody's *reflection*. He had stepped up beside me. Now, he smirked. "Nervous, Lieutenant?"

I considered shooting him, for good measure. "Stay here," I snapped. "Keep an eye out."

For what, Brody didn't ask.

I turned and walked around the side of the station. There was a Dumpster near a chain link fence in the back, overflowing with two days' worth of trash. I wasn't sure what I was looking for, but on the backside of the building, I found a red metal door labeled EMPLOYEES ONLY. The ground around it was littered with old cigarette butts. On a whim, I reached for the handle.

It turned.

"Brody!" I called out, softly.

A second later, Brody appeared. "What?" he said.

"The back door's unlocked."

With the hand that wasn't holding the gun, Brody scratched his nose. He looked as sun-scorched and miserable as I felt. Yet both of us hesitated, staring at the metal door. It should have, but this didn't feel like finding an oasis in the desert. "They might have a phone that works," Brody finally said.

I had been thinking that as well. After a moment, I nodded, and opened the door.

The interior hallway was pitch-black - windowless. With the beam of the flashlight cutting a pale circle ahead of us, I crept forward. Should we call out, I wondered? In case an employee was still around, and thought we were burglars?

We kept quiet.

We passed by the public restrooms. Their doors were propped open, shadows swimming in the deeper darkness. On the threshold of the station proper, we paused. Shelves spread out in neat aisles before the cash register. I clicked the flashlight off - plenty of daylight poured through the windows upfront; there was no need to waste batteries - I strode purposefully around behind the counter.

A phone hung on the wall above the register. I lifted the receiver to my ear, then shook my head. "No dial tone," I reported.

Brody looked less than stunned.

Nevertheless, we checked the phone in the small employee office, even the one back in the stockroom, which we had to navigate in near-total darkness. Even the flashlight didn't help much. Brody tripped over a large box just inside the door, cursing as his knee barked against the wall. Automatically, I shushed him. I felt like we needed to be quiet. There was a smell I couldn't quite place, that might have just been the milk in the freezer cases turning sour. It made me think of the time I had seen worms feasting on the eyes of a dead cat behind Scarcliff's dorms.

Brody snatched the receiver off the wall and dropped it back in its cradle. "Nothing," he said. "Not even static. What the hell is going on?"

"I don't know," I said, honestly. "I guess we should keep moving."

"I'm going to hit the head first," Brody said.

I nodded, swallowing my suggestion that he just relieve himself in the bushes. I didn't like being in here. Something felt - off.

I handed Brody the flashlight - "So you don't fall in the toilet when you're taking a piss," I said, and received a middle-fingered salute in response. While he disappeared down the hallway, I wandered up and down the aisles, out where there was enough light to see by. Down one row were bottles of whiskey, rum, tequila, and wine, their contents dark as blood in the dimness. Was this where Donovan had stopped to buy his last fifth of Jack Daniels? I ran my fingertips over the bottles. It was airless inside the store. Sweat was sliding down my sides from under my arms.

That reminded me. Near the counter was a display of hats - the sort of cheap, touristy crap that got sold at gas stations. Most of them had NASCAR emblems or the Virginia state logo on the brims. One, however, was basic camouflage. I plucked the tags off of it, tugged the cap down over my ears. Once this was all over, I would return to pay for it. For now, I needed something to keep the sun off my sca-

I would never be sure what, precisely, it was that I saw in that window behind me, as I was looking up into the little oval mirror on top of the hat stand; it was movement, I was certain of that, but when I spun around, bringing my rifle up, the parking lot was empty, washed clean of color by the unrelenting sun.

****

Peach Tree, Virginia, was a small town of approximately nine thousand souls tucked into a valley near an offshoot of the James River. Its main industry these days was a plastics factory on the far side of town, across the railroad tracks where the houses were small and grungy.

I had been to Peach Tree a few times, on school-sponsored outings to the movies or the local pizza parlor. Had this been a regular Fourth of July, Donovan would have driven Brody and I into town that evening to watch the fireworks, then taken us for burgers and fries at Peach Tree's twenty-four-hour diner afterwards. There was a Holiday Inn out by the Interstate where my father had stayed the one and only time had had visited me at Scarcliff, the day Colonel Thorne had presented me with my first lieutenant bars.

A red-white-and-blue HAPPY INDEPENDENCE DAY! banner stretched across Peach Tree's Main Street. True to its name, Main Street was Peach Tree's primary artery - what the highway into town became after passing by the local high school and some crumbling Victorian mansions on the edge of town. Those houses had all been dark and quiet, yards empty of people or dogs, as Brody and I had passed. We found the windows of the businesses along Main Street dark, as well. The signs in most of them read *closed*, but even inside the twenty-four-hour diner, the booths were empty, not a soul behind the counter. I was almost afraid to look inside. Afraid of what might be looking back at me from the other side of the glass.

I hadn't said a word to Brody about what I had seen, or not seen, back at the gas station.

"Where is everybody?" Brody asked. I just shook my head.

The town was completely silent.

Brody sat down on the hood of a Jeep parked along the curb. A few cars were stalled in the middle of Main Street, just as Donovan's truck had been back on the highway. None had the keys inside. We had checked. Brody slugged some water from one of the bottles in his rucksack, then offered it to me. I drank deeply. You had to be tough to withstand the daily P.T. drills at Scarcliff, one of the only military rituals Brody had never balked at, but it had still been a long, hot hike into town. I was footsore and sunburned. The sweat on Brody's cheeks had dried in salty tracks. "How do we find the sheriff's station?" he asked, crumpling the empty bottle up and pitching it into a trash can nearby.

"It's down that way." I pointed to the next intersection, adjacent to Peach Tree's yellow-brick courthouse. I had a good memory for landmarks and terrain. *Spatial intelligence*, Donovan had called it. "You okay to keep going?"

"Yeah." Though Brody looked a little pale to me, he rose, and stretched. "But I'm not sure we're going to find anybody once we get there."

Honestly, neither was I.

The silence grew louder as we walked further down the street. If Brody had noted the absence of birds, he didn't comment on it, yet I saw him glance uneasily at the upper stories of the brick-fronted shops we were passing. There were goosebumps on his arms, despite the heat. I had them, too, along with the unshakeable sense that, once again, someone, somewhere was watching us. "What about our weapons?" Brody asked, softly, as we turned the corner and the sheriff's station appeared halfway down the block. It stood across from the Civil War memorial on the courthouse lawn. A plastic bag was dancing there, riding currents of wind. The sound it made was like menacing laughter.

"What about them?" I half-hissed back. I had a death grip on my rifle.

"Is it such a good idea to walk in armed to a police station?"

I glared sideways at him. It had been Brody's idea - his insistence, in fact - to bring along the guns. Or had he forgotten that? "Keep that pistol out, Private," I growled.

For once, Brody didn't argue.

A single squad car was parked - rammed, practically - in front of the station's main entrance. The inside was dark. No emergency power, even, just like back at Scarcliff. I knew that couldn't be right; emergency services buildings always had backup generators. They were like hospitals in that way. The front door opened soundlessly when Brody pulled on it.

I went in first, sweeping the area with my flashlight. My finger rested on the rifle's trigger. "Hello?" I called out, softly.

Nobody answered.

Brody let the door fall shut. For a moment we stood stock-still, letting our eyes adjust to the darkness.

My heart was pounding in my ears.

A long counter split off from the main reception area. Beyond it were the deputies' desks, the sheriff's private office, and the dispatcher's radio station. That was what I made for, after checking that the phone behind the counter wasn't working. (It wasn't.) I played the flashlight over the radio's knobs and dials, wishing I knew more about these things - wondering if, like ham radios, it operated on its own battery power -

"Is that blood?" Brody whispered.

I turned around. My flashlight beam jumped - from Brody's blanched face, to the puddle he was staring at on the floor.

It was silvery, viscous-looking. Like oil, except I knew it wasn't. Something had clotted in my throat. I cleared it. "Do you see a trail leading away?" I asked.

Brody shook his head. In the dark, further shaded by the brim of his hat, his eyes were blue as crystals. "River, *what the fuck is going on*?"

"I don't know." I turned back to the radio, returning the rifle to my shoulder. Just like back on the quad with Donovan, some instinct I didn't fully understand was taking over, making it possible for me to think through the terror. "I'm pretty sure radios like these run on their own power. We should be able to get it working, if it isn't damaged..."

"Let me see that." Brody shouldered me aside. "Shine that light up here," he commanded. I, mostly out of surprise, complied; Brody flipped a lever on the side of the radio, fiddled with one of the knobs on the front, then started turning a dial at the top. He seemed to know what he was doing. I strained my ears, hoping to hear static, or better yet, voices; but after Brody had turned the dial left and right until it clicked several times, he gave up and shook his head. "It should be working, but it isn't. It's just like everything else, all the cars and all the phones and all the lights. Like something fried it." Only then did he seem to notice me staring at him. He folded his arms defensively. "What?"

"How do you know anything about radios?" I asked.

"And you don't, is that what you mean, Lieutenant?" I flushed. Brody smirked. "I did learn a few things before coming to Scarcliff. My old man owns a yacht. We used to take her out in the summers, sail up and down the New England coast. Any good skipper needs to know how to use a radio."

Had this been before or after the good Senator Brody packed his eldest son off to boarding school? I didn't ask. The dysfunctionality of Brody's family was none of my business. "Is there a way to fix it?" I asked.

"Beats me," Brody shrugged. "I said I knew how to use a radio, not how to build one. Do I look like MacGyver?"

"Who's MacGyver?"

"Are you being serious right now?" When I shrugged, Brody shook his head. "Your knowledge of pop culture," he declared, "is truly lacking." He glanced back at the pool of silvery stuff on the linoleum. "So? What now, fearless leader?"

I walked over to the window. Put my back to Brody. Rested my forearm against the glass, and stared across the street at the courthouse.

There was no use pretending any longer that what had happened at Scarcliff was an isolated incident. *Something* had happened inside this sheriff's station. I could still feel it, like the violence that had occurred here had left a sizzle in the air. And entire towns did not simply vanish, as the people in this one seemed to have.

Dead bodies did not get up and walk off by themselves.

We could go house to house, business to business, check for - I hated to think it, but the word that came to mind was "survivors." I didn't want to do that, though. From the moment we had set foot inside Peach Tree's city limits, every fiber of my being had been screaming that we needed to get the hell out of there. Watching the shadows grow long across the courthouse lawn, I found that feeling only intensified.

"I think we should keep going," I said, at last.

"Okay." Brody had thrown himself down in the dispatcher's chair. He rolled it back enough to stretch out his legs. "But go where, is the question? Just follow the road and hope we eventually wander back into civilization?"

"I think we should go to Fort Green," I said.

Brody looked away. Was he thinking of Sergeant Donovan - of how fragile the big man had looked, as we had covered his body with that tarp? "River, that's like fifty miles from here."

"Forty-three, to be exact," I said.

"Fifty, forty-three...It's kind of the same thing when you're humping it," Brody said.

I disagreed. I thought seven fewer miles was a pretty big deal when you were humping it. "What would you suggest we do, Brody? Wait around here and hope the cavalry shows up? Hope whatever happened to these people, to Donovan, doesn't happen to us? Do you think your old man might be sending in the Secret Service to rescue you?"

"I didn't say I had a better plan." Brody's voice was uncharacteristically humble. "But that doesn't mean yours will be easy."

"Yeah, well, not everything in life is easy," I said. I realized I was being an asshole, but I didn't care. "We should load up with as many supplies as we can while we're in town. But we need to hurry. I don't want to be here after dark."

Brody didn't ask me why that was.

There was a sporting goods store back on Main Street. In it, after Brody kicked in the back door - something he was surprisingly good at, I was noticing - with the aid of the flashlight we collected another rucksack for me, two ponchos, two bedrolls, some Cliff bars, packages of beef jerky, cans of dried fruit, and more bottles of water. We divided up the haul evenly between our packs, although Brody seemed to think, as the bigger and taller of our pair, he should carry more of the weight.

I also selected a hunting knife from the glass display case in the back of the store. I didn't say anything when Brody took down a twelve-gauge shotgun and a box of shells. I was thinking it might be a good idea to do some target practicing that evening, before Brody had to prove his claim that he could shoot in a firefight.

If he had to prove his claim.

Back out on the sidewalk, I was folding up the map I had taken from beside the checkout counter when Brody said, "There's a fallout shelter."

I looked at him. "What? Where?"

"Right down that alley." Brody was looking down the alley across the street from where we stood. It ran between two old, multiple-story brick buildings, one of which looked like it could have been a schoolhouse, back in the day. A yellow fallout shelter sign was fixed to the side of it. Its side door was ajar.

Had that door been open earlier? I couldn't remember. It was possible I might not have noticed it.

"Maybe we should check it out," Brody said.

He sounded less than certain. I, too, hesitated. *Leave now,* my brain was screaming. But what if the townspeople had assembled in their fallout area, based on some emergency bulletin Brody and I had missed while we were asleep in our dorm rooms back at Scarcliff? What if we were about to strike off on a forty-three-mile hike when help was literally beneath our feet? I shouldered my pack and bedroll, shoring up my nerve. "Just be quiet," I said, by way of caution, again not really knowing why. Again, Brody did not argue.

Being quiet turned out to be easier said than done. The stairwell leading down from the alley was metal. Our boots rang on every step. Three-quarters of the way down, Brody's shotgun - he had hooked it over his arm - glanced off the railing; the resultant noise was like the peal of a bell announcing our arrival. In the lead, I cringed and looked back at him.

"Sorry," Brody whispered.

Even in the dark, with just my flashlight to guide us, I could see the pulse beating in his throat. His shoulders blocked most of the sunlight stealing through the half-open door behind us. We had propped it open with our rucksacks and bedrolls, sharing the same, unspoken dread that a gust of wind would blow it shut, entombing us down here in the humid dark. I turned again, cautiously descending the last few steps.

At the bottom was an arched doorway, yawning like the mouth of a cave. There was no light whatsoever down here, natural or otherwise. My flashlight seemed a pitiable weapon against so much blackness. I remembered the feel of the darkness inside the dormitory stairwell back at Scarcliff, how it had seemed to contain its own gravity. This darkness was the same, wrapped around us like water. A cobweb brushed Brody's cheek. He cursed quietly as he swiped it aside.

I was staring straight ahead.

I wasn't sure, at first, what I was seeing. People, yes, but I thought - it would have been strange, as it was late afternoon, but I thought at first they were sleeping, piled together on the fallout shelter's floor. The ceiling, the walls (I saw, as I swept the flashlight beam around) were exposed brick, damp with condensation. The floor was concrete, barely an inch of it uncovered with - bodies. Hundreds and hundreds of bodies. Men, women, and children.

The only one I really saw, the only one I would later remember, was a woman. She was lying close to the foot of the stairs, like she had been trying to crawl back up them. Her arms were outstretched, fingers curled into claws; she was lying on her side, knees against her chest, black hair streaked with gray half-hiding her pale, contorted face. She wore a denim skirt and a short pink tank top. Her mouth was frozen into an *o*, and it was obvious immediately to me that she was dead - they were all dead, in my heart of hearts I knew it - though not so obvious what had killed her; there were no wounds, no blood other than a pinkish-white foam around the woman's lips and nose, the floor beneath her ear...Then I saw the blisters on her skin, and understanding hit me like a wave.

Brody was frozen on the last step behind me. I would think, later, how lost he had looked in that instant. There was no time for thinking anything then. I grabbed Brody's arm; Brody looked at me, shaken loose from the horror that had fallen over him; our eyes met; and at the same time, we pounded back up the stairs, escaping out into the daylight.

We did not stop running until we were more than a mile outside of town.

I threw my rucksack - the only thing I had paused to grab - against the base of an old, listing beech tree. I had not been thinking clearly when I had chosen our route out of town; a left turn past the plastics factory had taken us to a narrow two-lane stretch of blacktop closer to the railroad track than the Interstate. Off in the distance, I could see an old pickup rusting against a barbwire fence.

Brody slid his pack off his shoulders. Leaning over, he clasped his thighs with both hands, trying to catch his breath. "What...what could have done that to those people, River?"

"Poison," I said.

Brody looked up at me. Under his sunburn, his face was bloodless. "You mean like...like mustard gas?"

I nodded. Sitting down, I put my back against the beech tree's rough bark. My hair was plastered to my head beneath my stolen cap. I snatched the cap off, luxuriating in the feel of the wind caressing my scalp. "I mean, I doubt it *was* mustard gas, since that hasn't been used since, like, World War II, but something along those lines. Sarin, maybe. Or anthrax."

"Anthrax? Isn't that the stuff the Taliban mailed to the White House after 9/11?"

I sighed. "I think it got mailed to Congress. And I'm pretty sure it wasn't the Taliban behind it."

Brody seemed not to hear me. "Are we going to get sick from it?"

"I don't think so," I said. "The effects of something like that would be pretty immediate, and we were in town for an hour or so..."

"But - how could that happen to them?" Brody seemed unable to process this latest horror. He had begun pacing, up and down on the blacktop's gravel shoulder. I watched him. "They were inside a nuclear fallout shelter, for Christ's sake. Shouldn't that have protected them?"

Why did he expect me to have these answers? "Look," I said. "I don't know how it happened, or who was behind it, or why anybody would want to carry out a chemical attack on some place like Peach Tree, Virginia. I'm just telling you I think that's what happened."

Reaching into my rucksack, I yanked out a bottle of water and unscrewed the cap. Brody made a sound of protest. "Is it safe to drink that?"

I froze, the bottle almost to my lips. I looked down into it. The water *smelled* okay, like water always smelled, but the bottle had come from that sporting goods store on Peach Tree's Main Street. Could something like anthrax poison water, through plastic? Did I really want to find out? Carefully, I replaced the cap and threw the bottle onto the railroad tracks. "I guess we should throw out everything we picked up in town," I said, reluctantly. "The ponchos. The bedrolls. The food - all of it."

As if in protest, my stomach rumbled.

Brody plopped down beside me in the shade. To our west, the sun was an orange fireball sinking steadily into the horizon. The heat was soupy still, dusk probably an hour off. Crickets should have been singing in the meadows, but the evening was as unnaturally silent as the rest of this awful, strange day had been. "You're not going to like this," Brody warned me.

I groaned. "Now what?"

"Before we left Scarcliff, while you were up taking a shower, I may have gone back to the commissary and...liberated some of the snacks from the vending machines. And by 'liberated,' I mean I busted out the glass and stole everything inside."

I couldn't help it. A slow smile cracked the corners of my parched lips. "Tell me that included a Twix," I said.

****

It was not much of a feast. Nor did it seem possible that we could manage to do something as normal as eating, after what we had just seen. Yet somehow, they we were, and even as I thought about pictures I had seen of soldiers sitting on their tanks after a firefight, passing cans of C-rations back and forth and mugging for the camera, I had to admit things seemed less hopeless after I had scarfed down two granola bars (Brody had been at least somewhat practical in his thievery), two pieces of chocolate, and a bottle of Vitamin Water. Brody, using the rucksack he had brought from Scarcliff as a pillow, stretched out on the grass alongside the railroad track. "So what's the story with you and your old man?" he asked.

"What story?"

My tone was innocent. Brody kicked some pebbles toward me. The railroad track was lined with them. "C'mon, man. I'm not stupid. Nobody stays at school year-round just 'cause they're dad's too busy to spend time with them."

"My mother died." I was not entirely comfortable sharing this with Kyle Brody. But, he had asked, and the answer just sort of - came out. "Right before I enrolled at Scarcliff, three years ago. My father was never a very demonstrative guy, but without her around...He just didn't know what to do with me. I guess he still doesn't. It's easier for us both if I just stay away."

"That sucks," Brody said.

I shrugged and stretched my legs out, fingers laced behind my head. "What about you? What's your story?"

"What story?"

"Har har," I said. "Why'd your parents ship you off to boarding school? Isn't your dad a totally devoted family man?"

"Piece of advice," Brody said. "Don't believe everything you hear on Fox News." I got my news from the BBC, actually, but I didn't feel the need to tell Brody that. "My old man's a prick," he said, blithely. "He talks a good game for the voters, all about love and honesty and 'family values,' but he cheats on my mom all the time. And she just lets him. She gets mad because I won't play along with the one-big-happy-family fiction. It's like she thinks I can't hear her crying through the wall." Brody looked away, like he had said too much. "Anyway. Like you said. It's just easier to stay away."

I nodded. I wasn't sure what to say. I didn't think my situation really compared to Brody's. My father had been crazy about my mother. In all the ways he was capable of, he had shown her that. Even with the globe-trotting and constant uprooting that came with being a military family, my life at home had been a happy one, while Mom was alive. Even now, I knew my father loved me. He was one of the reasons why I worked so hard at Scarcliff.

Maybe, I thought, Brody's father was one of the reasons why he didn't.

Rolling onto his elbow, Brody looked at me. He had taken off his hat. His hair had dried in unruly spikes. I wondered what my hair looked like. I would have given just about anything for a shower. "River, do you think this is really terrorists?"

One of us had had to put it into words, eventually.

By now, twilight was falling over the treetops. Soon, the sun would disappear into her bed. I had already tossed out the rucksack I had taken from town, along with everything that might have been contaminated inside of it - except for the hunting knife, which I had tucked down in my boot, and Brody's shotgun and extra shells. Those I was willing to run the risk of holding onto. "I think it would be pretty difficult for terrorists to carry out an attack like this," I said, carefully. "Releasing nerve gas in a subway or a building is one thing. Taking out an entire town *and* its power grid is something else." Not to mention stealing bodies in broad daylight, without leaving behind any trace of a trail...

"Maybe the army took the power out," Brody suggested. "Like, they cut the power lines and the phone lines to keep the affected area quarantined."

"Yeah, but why would they?" I asked. "Chemical weapons aren't contagious. Sarin or anthrax aren't like viruses. You have to encounter the poison directly, like by inhaling it, to get sick. Once the poison disperses, there's nothing to worry about."

"Maybe they were trying to keep a lid on what happened. Prevent a public panic. Or - "

"Or?" I said, keenly.

"Or maybe the army did it," Brody said. "Like a - a test, or something."

He blushed, having at least enough decency to be embarrassed for suggesting that the military my father was a part of would massacre thousands of its own citizens. "I don't think even the army would be dumb enough to test out a chemical weapon on American soil," I said. "Besides, a military weapons test wouldn't explain what happened to Donovan."

"What do you think did happen to Donovan?"

"Honestly?" I shrugged. "I have no idea. But we've wasted enough time wondering about it," I added, standing up, "so let's hit the road while there's still some daylight left."

By cutting across the field where the pickup was rusting against the fence, divested of engine and tires - which was too bad, Brody commented, like a real gearhead; a truck as old as that might still have run after an EMP, since it wasn't powered by a computer - we soon came back to the highway. The town of Peach Tree was just rooftops on the smoke-gray horizon. The wind was blowing the leaves silver-side-up. I had lived in Virginia long enough to know a rain was coming. Shame we'd had to throw away those ponchos, I reflected, eyeing the clouds banking off to the east. A distant sprig of lightning lit them from beneath, followed by a growl of thunder.

The silent power lines above our heads sighed in the breeze.

"We should find someplace to get indoors," Brody said, holding his hat on his head with one hand. "I don't like my chances of not getting struck by lightning. Not the way this day is going." I couldn't keep from laughing.

In less than a mile, we came to a rest stop - one that was, unsurprisingly by this point, dark and deserted. Three cars were parked in the lot. Brody looked inside each one, and reported that the keys were all gone. I held my breath as he opened the glass double doors. He stood aside for me to shine the flashlight around. I gave the faux-marble lobby a quick once-over, noting the vending machines to one side, a shuttered information booth, some payphones in the corner.

"Looks clear," I said.

The first raindrops struck the roof as the door closed behind us. That was when the thing crouching in the shadows stood up.

****

Brody would have shot the man if I hadn't grabbed the shotgun, aiming its barrel at the payphones. "Don't shoot!" the man shouted, throwing up his hands.

"Jesus!" Brody cursed under his breath. I raised an eyebrow at him, silently asking if he was cool. Brody nodded. He looked shaken. I let go of the shotgun.

"We're not going to shoot you," I said, quickly. "We were just looking for a place to get in out of the rain."

The man took a timid step forward, into the circle of brightness cast by my flashlight. He was middle-aged, bald, and flabby, dressed in khaki high-waisted shorts and a pinstripe polo. Sweat stood out across his brow. He kept his hands up, like we were old-fashioned robbers in a stick-up. His eyes went round as they looked first at Brody and then at me. "You're just kids," he said, incredulously. "You can't be soldiers!"

Brody and I glanced down simultaneously at our white tee-shirts, camouflage trousers, and combat boots. Not to mention Brody's twelve-gauge, my M16, and the Beretta stuck in Brody's waistband... "We're cadets, at Scarcliff Academy," I explained. "It's a military school, on the other side of Peach Tree." It was clear from the man's expression he had never heard of the town, or the school. "Does one of those cars out there belong to you, sir?"

"N-no." Slowly, the man lowered his hands. Two more figures had risen up behind him. One was a woman in her forties wearing a green cotton dress. She had mousy brown hair and a pinched-looking mouth. The other was a girl, maybe fifteen, maybe sixteen, in cut-off denim shorts and an American flag tee-shirt. She had dark skin and eyes shaped like almonds. I was instantly aware of how gross and sweaty I was, and how much shorter compared to Brody. "We were passing by on the Interstate late last night when our van stalled. We walked down here to find a phone - we couldn't get a signal on our cell phones - but the payphones were all out. There were some other folks here with us for a while, but they decided to try walking to the nearest town this morning."

Brody exchanged a look with me. We had seen no one on the road to or from Peach Tree. Of course, they could have gone the other direction, I told myself.

The woman moved a step away from her husband. I assumed they were married, anyway. The girl was staring at Brody. Naturally. "Are you boys all right?" the woman asked, anxiously.

How were we supposed to answer that, after everything we had been through in the past twelve hours? I said, "We have some food, if you'd like something to eat."

The woman looked like she might fall to her knees and thank God for us.

The man and woman introduced themselves as Mr. and Mrs. Keller of Kansas City, Kansas. They had been driving to Washington, D.C., for the holiday weekend. Mr. Keller related this while Brody distributed our last bottles of uncontaminated water. The vending machines had been picked clean by the overnighters. Understandably, they hadn't wanted to set out without supplies, although it seemed to me they could have left the Kellers with *something*.

Mr. Keller put his back against the wall, his arm around his wife. Mrs. Keller kept toying with the gold cross around her neck. Rain beat a jagged symphony against the windows, punctuated by cymbal crashes of thunder and lightning. Brody and I were sitting cross-legged with our weapons across our knees.

The girl smiled at Brody when he handed her a Snickers.

"We figure the state police or someone will be by here soon," Mrs. Keller was saying, nervously, turning her candy bar over in her hands without unwrapping it. "I just can't imagine what could have caused such a widespread power outage..."

"How far is your school from here, did you say?" Mr. Keller asked.

Brody was looking at me, like *we have to tell them.* "About fifteen miles," I said, and then, "But listen..."

Between the two of us, we told the Kellers everything. Waking up to the power and phone outage. Sergeant Donovan dying of his wounds on the quad. His body disappearing. The people we had discovered in Peach Tree's fallout shelter. The silvery blood on the sheriff's station floor. Mrs. Keller had both hands pressed over her mouth by the time we finished. Mr. Keller just looked at us solemnly. "Well, it's a good thing you boys found us," he said, gravely. "I don't know what's going on out there, but it's no place for children on their own. You can stay here with us until help arrives. We'll look after you. Won't we, sweetheart?" He gave his wife's shoulders a reassuring squeeze.

He wasn't getting it. "Mr. Keller," I said, politely, "sir, Brody and I appreciate that. We do. But I'm not sure help is coming. And something may - still be out there." The rain drumming against the windows seemed to get louder. That had to be my imagination. Didn't it? "As soon as the storm passes, we're following the Interstate north to Fort Green. It's a long walk, but you and your family are welcome to come with us."

"We have weapons," Brody put in, gamely. "We won't let anything happen to you. I promise."

"Now boys." Mr. Keller shook his head. "Listen to yourselves! Whatever has happened, the government is not just going to abandon its citizens. They'll send the National Guard in, if they have to. The best thing we can do," he said, speaking right over my protest, "is stay put until they get here."

"And if they don't get here?" Brody said, almost angrily.

"There's no need to think like tha, son." Mr. Keller smiled tightly, as if to say the matter was closed. "Now, I think we could all do with some sleep."

I got up. I walked into the men's room, feeling my way along the wall, not wanting to waste the flashlight. How in God's name had people found their way around before light bulbs? *It was called candlelight, Lieutenant,* I heard Donovan say, and grinned weakly at the shadowed reflection of myself in the mirror above the men's room sink.

The door opened as I was splashing water on my cheeks. Brody barged in. He was livid. "Can you believe that asshole?" he said, in a furious whisper. "He's out there trying to convince me we probably panicked and didn't see what we thought we saw in town. He wants to stay here, with no food, no water, and wait for fucking FEMA to - "

"He's scared," a soft voice said.

I nearly jumped sideways into the urinals.

The girl had slipped into the bathroom silently. She leaned back against the door, hands folded behind her. The end of a long black ponytail hung over one of her shoulders. Out in the lobby, I could hear her parents arguing quietly. They probably hadn't noticed she was in here with two strange boys. Yet. "Last night, out on the Interstate, just before our car went dead," she said. Brody and I were both gaping at her. "We saw lights up in the sky. Blue lights, moving fast. I'd never seen anything

39

like it. They were too low to the ground to be from a satellite, and they weren't moving like the lights on a plane or a helicopter. Then there was this bright orange glow off to the north and west, and a split-second later, our van just stopped running."

She made a sweeping motion with her hand, as if wiping the van, and its engine, off the map.

Prickles had begun walking up and down my spine. The darkness inside the restroom felt absolute. A flash of lightning showed us in all a sudden tableau: the girl, lean and coltish, pressed back against the door; me, crowded up against the sink; Brody, standing with his arms crossed, effortlessly cool and macho. The girl was looking at him like I wasn't even in the room. And to think, for maybe five seconds back there, I had almost started to *like* Kyle Brody. "What did the people who were with you last night think about all of this?" he asked.

"They saw the glow in the sky, too. They thought we were crazy for hanging around this morning. This one guy, he was an ex-Navy Seal. He said the best way to survive would be to keep moving." The girl paused. "He called it an invasion."

I tried not to shudder. I cleared my throat. "You could try talking to your dad - "

"Do you think I haven't?" The girl finally looked at me. I felt the color come up in my cheeks and looked down at my boots. Part of me still couldn't believe this was happening. That I wasn't going to wake up back in my dorm room at Scarcliff with a weird-ass dream to tell Donovan about at the fireworks that evening. "He won't listen to me, or to Mom. He's too scared."

"What's your name?" Brody asked, abruptly.

The girl ducked her chin. I was sure she was blushing. "Cheyenne," she said, softly. Of course it was, I thought, not very nicely. Because that was the perfect name for the adopted Chinese daughter of the sort of white, Midwestern couple who would drive halfway across the country to celebrate Independence Day in the nation's capital. "Cheyenne," Brody said, "you should come with us. Even if they won't."

Cheyenne's chin snapped up. "I - I couldn't do that - "

"Cheyenne? Honey?" The door squeaked; Mr. Keller's moon-shaped face appeared around it. Cheyenne jumped back guiltily. Mr. Keller glanced between the three of us, frowning. "What are you kids doing in here?"

"We were just talking, Daddy." Cheyenne threw us a look somewhere between apologetic and embarrassed. *Dads*, it seemed to mean.

Still, I wondered if Mr. Keller hadn't overheard us. He looked coldly again at Brody, motioning Cheyenne over to him. "Come on, honey," he said. "Let's let the boys clean up in peace..."

The door fell shut on the rest of his words. Brody stared at it for a moment, then turned around and smacked his palm, hard, against the wall. "Idiot," I heard him breathe out, between his teeth.

I did not disagree. But there wasn't much we could do to save someone who didn't want to be saved. "I'll keep first watch," I said. "You should get some sleep. No matter what they decide, you and I are leaving as soon as this storm blows through."

Brody nodded. He was looking down at his boots, jaw set in a hard line.

I looked back at him once as I went out. I thought he was looking at himself in the mirror, his expression caught between fury and helplessness.

In the dark, of course, it was possible I imagined it.

5 July

The beach was no place I had ever been in waking life - at least, not that I remembered. The sand was wet and thick, like concrete. My feet had sunk into it up to the ankles. Waves crashing against the shore filled my ears with a dull, relentless roar. I tasted salt on my lips, felt the sting of the hot, hot sun on my cheeks and back.

A woman in a white sundress was walking toward me. I could hear her laughing, an odd, disjointed sound, like a recording that had begun to degrade; she was holding a wide-brimmed hat on her head, as the breeze tried to snatch it away. Her voice drifted to me as if coming from some great distance. *River! River!*

The longing that rushed up in my chest was palpable. "Mom?" I whispered.

The sun was right behind her. But something was wrong. It was too bright. The sky that should have been blue was darkening to orange. As I watched, my feet trapped in the sand, my mother turned. My eyes were burning. It was a moment before I realized I wasn't crying; my eyes were *actually* burning, the jelly inside of them superheating to a boil. The sky was on fire, tongues of flame swooping down from orange and black clouds; I heard my mother screaming, felt the flesh start to melt right off my bones -

"River. River, man, you're dreaming. Wake up."

I cried out.

Brody snatched his hand back from my shoulder. I stared up at him, heart thundering in my chest. Brody's features came together slowly: straight nose, planed cheeks, strong jaw. I was lying on the faux-marble floor of the rest stop lobby. Brody was crouched over me, rucksack already on his back.

"The storm's gone through," he said.

I sat up. My throat was dry; I could taste salt on my lips. I swiped at my cheeks with the back of my hand, hoping he hadn't seen the dampness on them. "What time is it?" I asked hoarsely.

"I dunno. Late."

So it was. A glance out the glass doors showed me a crescent moon suspended over the treetops, a blue-black sky sprinkled liberally with stars. Mr. and Mrs. Keller hovered anxiously in the corner. Mrs. Keller looked like she wanted to prevent us from leaving, but she didn't know how. I smiled at her. The Kellers were nice people. They didn't deserve for this awfulness to be happening to them.

The girl, Cheyenne, was sound asleep beneath the payphones, black hair like spilled ink across her shoulders.

Mr. Keller walked us out as far as the edge of the parking lot. Brody and I had both tried again to convince him to come with us. He had politely but firmly refused. "If you just follow the road up this way," he said, pointing, "you'll come to the Interstate. But I still think you would be better off just waiting..."

"Thanks, Mr. Keller. We'll be all right." Shifting the rifle to my other arm, I offered him my hand. He looked into my eyes as he shook it. His jaw was tight, like he was holding back some powerful emotion.

He shook Brody's hand, as well. "We won't forget about you," Brody promised. "As soon as we make it to Fort Green, we'll send back help."

"You boys be careful out there," Mr. Keller said.

He stepped back onto the sidewalk, arms folded across the slope of his gut. When I looked back, I could still see him standing there, hemmed in by shadows.

The night was very dark.

It was more than the kind of darkness you just weren't used to, with street lights and whatnot to chase it off. It was the same sort of darkness I had felt at Scarcliff and again in that fallout shelter beneath Peach Tree's Main Street - a darkness that carried its own weight. I noticed Brody scanning the trees to either side of us as we started up a deserted exit ramp onto the Interstate. The cool scent of fresh rain and wet leaves filled our noses. The breeze was almost a caress.

"How much food and water do we have left?" I asked.

Brody, who had insisted on carrying our one remaining rucksack, adjusted the straps across his shoulders. "Five granola bars and six bottles of water. I refilled all of them at the bathroom tap."

Split two ways, it wasn't much. "The food we can ration," I said. "The water - "

"Won't be enough to take us forty-three miles," Brody said.

"It's more like thirty-nine now," I offered. In the darkness, I saw him grin. "Listen - "

"It's all right, Lieutenant."

I did not like the resignation in Brody's voice. Turning around, I walked backwards up the ramp, facing him. "You don't even know what I was going to say."

"Sure I do. You were going to say we didn't have any choice but to leave those people behind. And anyway, since you're my commanding officer, *I* didn't leave them behind. You did."

"I didn't realize you were taking orders from me again, Private."

"I'm not." Brody's tone was not unfriendly. "But you could at least give me a field commission."

"To what? Lieutenant Colonel?" Brody laughed. I turned, facing forward again. We could ill afford for me to break an ankle. "I hate to break this to you, man, but lieutenants don't have the authority to promote our underlings. In the grand scheme of things, I'm a grunt, just like you are. But tell you what. The next time I see my father, I'll recommend he put you up for the Presidential Medal of Valor, or something."

"Awesome," Brody said.

We had reached the Interstate - another long black stretch of nothing, four lanes divided by a grassy median. The darkness didn't feel quite so thick out in the open. It was still pitch-black, however. We could have passed by entire cities in the distance, and I would never have known it.

Occasionally we came upon a car or van or pickup stopped in the middle of the road. There was never anyone around them, no sound other than the wind and the crunch of our boots on the asphalt. I had never appreciated before just how *loud* the modern world was.

Brody said, "Are you worried about him?"

"My father?" Brody nodded. I shrugged. "I mean, sure. In the abstract. But I can't imagine this thing has reached as far as D.C." I did not define what this "thing" was.

"Why is that?" Brody looked around, at the shadows pooled like dark water on the shoulders of the Interstate. Out here, all alone, it did seem possible we were the only two people left on the planet.

"Because D.C. has missile defense systems," I said.

"When did missiles come into this?" Brody's tone was sharp.

"What that girl described, back at the rest stop," I said. "The blue lights she and her family saw, from up here on the road."

"You mean Cheyenne?"

Of course the girl was the part of that statement Brody would focus on. "Whatever her name was," I said. Like I didn't recall her name perfectly well. "She said they saw blue lights, too low to be from a satellite, moving too fast to be from an aircraft. Right after that, the northwest sky lit up orange, and their van and their cell phones died. Sounds like a missile strike to me. You were the one who said we were probably looking at the aftermath of an EMP. That would accompany a missile strike."

"But those people, back in town - "

"Chemical weapons can be delivered by rockets or missiles, too. It's not like you have to put on a gas mask and go lob an aerosol canister in the street." Had this guy *never* read our JROTC field manual?

"So you're saying somebody nuked the East Coast of the United States?"

Brody had stopped walking. Understanding dawned on me, and I stammered, "I'm - I'm sure your family in Boston - "

" - is fine because Boston has missile defense systems." Brody sounded less than convinced. A guilty blush stole up over the collar of my tee-shirt. I had momentarily forgotten Brody had family out there, as well. "If somebody launched a nuclear weapon that close to here, shouldn't you and I be crispy critters right now?"

"It didn't have to be nuclear," I said. "It could have been a neutron device. Much smaller blast radius, much less property damage, limited radioactive fallout. Same body count." That was practically verbatim from something Donovan had said to our class once. Brody must have been staring out the window or doodling peace signs in his notebook that day.

"And you think this neutron missile, or whatever, got launched at Fort Green."

I nodded. I felt clammy underneath my clothes. Nights in Virginia weren't supposed to turn off cold like this during the summer. "You said you heard on the TV that the president was there, for the July Fourth weekend. Donovan could have seen the explosion on his way back from town and realized what had happened. Terrorists - "

"So we're back to terrorists, is it?" Brody's voice had gone hard, bitter-edged. What I could see of his face in the dark looked twisted. "Tell me something, Lieutenant. If you really believe Fort Green was vaporized, why are we still walking in that direction?"

"Because that's where the military will be setting up its defenses." I said it simply. Brody's lips parted, like he was about to make some smartass comment; for once, none seemed to occur to him. He closed his mouth. "Any strike against a military target on United States soil would bring out whatever remained of our military in force. It's only been about twenty-four hours since this thing went down. They're probably still assessing damage to civilian targets. That's why they haven't gotten here yet. But if we keep going, we'll eventually run into them - "

"Now you sound like Mr. Keller," Brody said, derisively. I flushed. "There's just one problem with your theory, Lieutenant. If the military is scrambling all of its forces toward Fort Green, why haven't we heard a single plane or helicopter pass over in the last twenty-four hours?"

That had not occurred to me.

What had occurred to me was that my perfectly rational explanation did not account for Sergeant Donovan's body disappearing from the quad, or all of the birds and animals and even insects vanishing, or the icy, oppressive sense of being watched that had come over me so often in the last few hours. That feeling had descended on me once more. The darkness seemed to be drifting, moving around us like currents at sea. Some nameless dread rested so heavily on my chest I could barely breathe. And still, I was loathe to let my theory go. "Okay," I said, challengingly. "What do you think it was she saw, Brody?"

"I - "

It was as much as he ever got to say.

I felt the vibrations first. They were like a low rumble beneath our feet. There was no sound; the night was perfectly, completely silent, yet the fine hairs on the backs of my arms stood straight up, as though a current of electricity had passed over us. Brody's eyes were huge, his knuckles white on the Beretta he had pulled free of his waistband. He was feeling it, too.

"Come on." I didn't know why I whispered that, but I grabbed Brody's arm and dragged him off the Interstate. A steep embankment fell down to a small scrub field on our right; we slipped and slid down into the mud, ending up on our knees in waist-high weeds. I could smell damp soil, wet grass. I eased the rifle down off my shoulder and peered back up onto the road.

In daylight, strangely, the shimmering triangle probably would have been invisible, dismissed as a current of air, or a shadow, if nothing else. In the dark, I could just see the object, whatever it was, hovering some ten feet above the ground. It was the size of a Frisbee, passing slowly over the Interstate. Like it was looking for something.

One second it was there. The next second, it had vanished.

Brody started to speak. I clutched his arm tighter. I was still staring up the rise at the Interstate. All of the blood in my body seemed to have frozen, right inside my veins.

Something was standing on the roadside. Lit by moonlight, it seemed to glow; its skin was white as alabaster, but not waxy-looking, and not hard, not like stone. The closest thing I could think of was soapstone, recalling, for some reason, the tribal African figurines my mother used to display in one of her innumerable curio cases.

Like those figurines, this creature looked - sculpted. It did not seem entirely alien. More than anything it seemed old, older than the oldest living being, like something that had been here before there were trees or rivers or mountains. It stood taller even than Brody, eight or possibly even nine feet, naked head to toe, hairless, poreless, broad-chested, with arms and legs like tree trunks and a brow ridge that, in profile, seemed unusually pronounced. Its neck was thick. Its nose was straight and sharp. Even from a distance, I could see that its ears were shaped perfectly, like sea shells. Almost delicate.

It was awesome.

It was terrifying.

It was not human.

How long the creature stood there, head cocked as though listening, I would never be sure. Only when it at last moved on down the Interstate, bare feet touching the ground without so much as a whisper, did I realize I still had the rifle pressed against my shoulder. As though I had been ready, all along, to fire.

"I think we should find someplace to hide when it gets daylight," I said.

Brody, walking beside me, nodded curtly.

It had been my decision for us to parallel the Interstate from the meadows and small stands of trees alongside it. It made for slower going, as the undergrowth this far out in the boondocks was thick as jungle fauna, but after what we had witnessed, staying out in the open seemed suicidal.

Traveling under cover of darkness, I had reasoned, would offer us some concealment from whatever was out there, hunting down survivors. Plus, it would be a lot less miserable to sleep somewhere cool while the sun was out.

Brody had not said much for an hour or so. After the whatever-it-was had walked away, I had looked over to discover him lying belly-down next to me in the weeds, Beretta trained up the embankment just as my rifle had been. Neither of us had said anything. We had just collected ourselves, and started walking.

What did you say, upon discovering your planet had been invaded by aliens?

All that was spinning in my mind were questions. What was the half-invisible, triangle-shaped object we had seen? Some kind of advanced weapon - something equipped to shoot poisonous gas at humans, maybe? Maybe. But there had been something about it, something that had chilled me even more than the alien itself. I kept thinking it was like some kind of drone, like the UAVs - Unmanned Aerial Vehicles - the army used to scout hostile terrain overseas. Had it, or something like it, been the thing I had felt watching us over the past twenty-four hours?

But if it could see us, why hadn't it seen us there along the road? And what about the fate of Fort Green? What the hell was I leading Brody and myself toward? Had the missile launch I was convinced Cheyenne and her parents had seen carried out been conducted by our invaders, or had the military realized one of our bases was being overrun and launched a counterattack? How many of those creatures might be waiting up ahead of us? How difficult would it be to take them down?

"Where do you think they came from?" Brody asked.

I glanced up in surprise, wondering for a moment if I had begun posing my questions out loud. I didn't think so. Brody just wasn't capable of shutting up for very long. "Who cares where they came from?" I said, ducking a low-hanging branch; the strand of trees we were navigating through seemed to be thickening. I glanced to my right, being sure we hadn't lost sight of the flat black ribbon that was the Interstate, unspooling under moonlight. "All I care about is getting them off our planet."

"Right," said Brody. "Nuke the bastards. 'Cause that always solves everything..."

"Okay, Senator Brody," I said, not very nicely. "I didn't notice you trying out your diplomacy skills back there."

"What was I supposed to do - hold up my hands and say, 'We come in peace'?" I almost laughed at that. "I'm not saying we invite them to tea at the White House. Assuming the White House is still standing. But that doesn't mean it wouldn't make sense to try learning about them. A peaceful solution always saves more lives than a military one, in the end."

For some reason, this statement, true as it was, annoyed me. "Yeah, well, you just keep on hoping for your peaceful solution," I said. "I'm going to keep hoping we hear some tanks rolling down the Interstate." Stepping over a broken branch, I couldn't stop myself from blurting out, "Or have you forgotten what those things did to Sergeant Donovan?"

"Of course I haven't forgotten." Brody's tone was measured. Another blush crept up on me, this one guilty-feeling. I preferred Brody being a jackass to Brody being reasonable and mature. "I liked Donovan, too, all right? I felt bad for how messed up he was from being over in Iraq - "

"Afghanistan," I said, stiffly. "He served two tours in Afghanistan."

"And he came back messed up," Brody said, like that was all that mattered. "I always thought that was a shame. You could tell he was a cool guy. He was too good for that." Brody pulled up, beneath the sheltering arms of a twisted maple, and fished a bottle of water for each of us out of his rucksack. The night had grown close and humid again after the alien and its drone-weapon thingy had disappeared. "I always thought *you* were too good for that," Brody said.

My eyebrows went up. "You think I'm too good to fight for my country?"

"Please don't give me that patriotic bullshit," Brody said, wearily. "I've seen how smart you are, man. The smartest person in our class, easily. You know how to think for yourself, and you aren't afraid to act when something is in front of you that needs dealing with. But the second you put on that cadet uniform, you shut your brain off. It's all, 'yes sir,' 'no sir,' 'what are your orders, sir?' You're too good for that," Brody swiped the back of his hand across his mouth, "and you're too good to get blown up in some stupid war because an asshole like my old man in Congress decides to start one, probably so he can get a kickback on a weapons contract."

"I should have known this would come back to your daddy issues," I said.

It was a nasty thing to say. I knew it before I said it. Something closed off in Brody's face. He straightened up, stowing the empty bottle back in his rucksack. His shoulders were stiff. "I want to go back," he said.

For a second, I thought he meant to Scarcliff. Then I realized, and shook my head. "Brody, there's no point. They made their decision."

"But now we've - "

"Now we've what? Seen an alien?" It was the first time either of us had spoken the word out loud. I saw Brody bite his lip. "Mr. Keller didn't want to believe us before, Brody. He's not going to start believing us now. It's not like we have any proof."

"So, what? We just leave them, knowing what's out there? I mean, Jesus, River." Brody's tone was disgusted. "We didn't even leave them with a weapon. You're so into being a soldier. Isn't it the job of a soldier to protect the innocent?"

"What do you want me to do, Brody? Take them hostage at gunp- "

A twig snapped.

I whirled around. My heart was in my throat. The tall weeds at our backs were rustling - Jesus-fucking-Christ it was dark out here - I brought the rifle up to my shoulder - sweat was rolling down my forehead, stinging my eyes - what if I couldn't see it, what if it could turn invisible or disappear, what if I never saw it coming for me until it -

"Don't shoot!" Brody practically shouted.

My finger twitched away from the trigger. I cursed, too loudly for the stillness.

Brody had darted forward, directly into my line of fire, throwing himself in front of something in the grass. A second later, I saw what it was. A dog.

A yellow Labrador retriever, to be exact. The dog looked all right, just muddy. Whining, he licked Brody's hand. "Where'd he come from?" I demanded, irritably. I wasn't irritated with the dog. But if I had shot it, or Brody...

"It's a she," Brody corrected me. He was stroking the dog's head, murmuring soothingly to him. Her. It. Whatever. "She has tags on," he said.

Great, I felt like saying. *We'll just call her owners to come pick her up.* "Look, Brody, we can't take care of a dog. We barely have enough food and water to keep *us* on our feet."

"We aren't leaving her out here." There was no argument to be brooked with Brody's tone. He stood, beaming down at the dog. The dog, like all females, gazed adoringly up at him. "Do you live around here, girl? You live near here? Where's home?"

At the word "home," the dog barked and bounded off into the weeds. After a few feet, she stopped, looking back at us with her tongue lolling out of her mouth.

"I think she wants us to follow her," Brody said.

I clenched my hands into fists; released them slowly; and counted silently to ten before answering. "Brody," I said, patiently, "we have a lot of ground to cover before we reach Fort Green. We can't go chasing some stray dog through the woods. I'm sorry."

There might have been more behind that apology than what I was willing to acknowledge. From the corner of my eye, I saw the edge of Brody's mouth curl up, like he was smirking. Then again, smirking was Brody's default expression. "If she does live near here, there might be people who could help us out," he said. "At the very least we could scrounge some supplies. Like you said. It's a long walk to Fort Green." He paused. "So? What do you want to do, Lieutenant?"

I looked from the dog, panting in the underbrush, to Brody, half-swallowed by the darkness under the trees. "Does this mean you're taking orders from me now?" I asked.

"Would you like to gloat about it," Brody said, "or do you want to make a decision?"

I grinned.

****

"This may have been a bad idea," Brody said.

From the shelter of the tree line, we were looking out across a neat row of fenced-in backyards. A subdivision. Judging by the size of the houses, a wealthy subdivision.

Before Scarcliff, I had spent my entire life on army bases. I knew in the abstract that the more crime, pollution, and homelessness became a problem in the cities, the further afield those with the means to do so moved. Along the Interstate corridor around Charlottesville, there had to be hundreds of housing communities just like this one, with manicured lawns and backyard patios and tree-lined avenues, home to moms and dads who commuted to jobs in the cities. Close by there would be some generic little town a bit larger than Peach Tree, with good schools, a street full of churches, and probably a shopping mall.

That town could have been five miles away from where we were, or fifteen. In the suburbs, the car was God. Suburbanites didn't even talk in terms of distance. They talked in terms of time. I had heard it from my classmates at Scarcliff - the ones born and raised in the U.S. *How far are you from Philadelphia? About forty-five minutes.* As in, the length of time it would take to drive there in mommy or daddy's SUV.

Unfortunately, those SUVs seemed to be just really big paperweights now, parked in the driveways of the subdivisions McMansion's. Forget aliens, I thought. People were going to die by the thousands just from a lack of basic necessities if this disaster proved to be widespread enough. Suburbs like this one would become like desert islands, the people in them, without their vehicles, as stranded as castaways, without access to food, water, or medicine.

The aliens were still a pressing concern, obviously.

As it happened to be the dead of night, it was not surprising that all of the houses we could see were quiet. Still, I did not think the residents were simply sleeping. None of the street lights were working, and the front door of the big brick ranch on the corner was thrown wide open; backpacks, purses, and suitcases littered the yards and gutters, as though people had started fleeing with their possessions only to realize how hard it was just to keep your own feet moving in the July heat. I hoped that was what had happened here, at least. A voluntary evacuation was better than the alternative.

I didn't see any bodies.

That didn't necessarily mean anything.

Moonlight had turned the grass from green to silver. I reached down, absently patting the dog's head. She licked my fingers. "Do you think she knows which house is hers?" I asked.

"I'm sure she does. She's a smart girl." Brody had holstered his Beretta in favor of the shotgun. Pushing his hat back - I had turned my cap around backwards, now that I didn't need it to keep the sun off of my face - he said, "If you think we should head back to the Interstate..."

"No." I was determined. "We need supplies. You were right."

"Sorry. Would you mind repeating that?"

I grinned, with my head turned so Brody couldn't see it. "You heard me, Private. Now come on. I don't like being out in the open like this. We don't know what might be watching."

Brody nodded. To the dog, he said, "All right, girl. *Home.*"

The dog bounded off.

We had to run to keep up with her. Rifle in hand, I nearly tripped over a tricycle tipped over sideways in a yard. I righted myself and kept running, skirting the picket fence of a white two-story with a wraparound porch, sprinting up the front walk of a gray split-level. A Lincoln Navigator was parked in front of the split-level's three-car garage. Brody was already standing at the front door as I drew even with the front steps, trying to catch my breath. "Where's the dog?" I asked.

"She went around back. I assume there's a doggie door."

Brody said this without reaching for the doorknob. What was he waiting for? I glanced uneasily down the dark, empty street. Shadows slid toward us across the lawn. The wind had picked up again, tossing the leaves of the trees in the split-level's front yard. "Well?" I said, in a whisper. "Shall we?"

"I feel like..." Brody glanced back at me. "Should we knock, or something?"

"Move," I hissed, impatiently. Elbowing Brody aside, I twisted the doorknob, honestly expecting it to be locked.

The door swung open soundlessly.

The entryway was dark. I supposed that went without saying, yet sixteen years of habit conspired to make me reach for the light switch inside the door. I flipped it. Nothing happened. *Stupid.* Glancing back at Brody - his mouth was thin, his shotgun raised - I clicked the flashlight on.

A stairwell to our right climbed up to the house's second story. To our left, another one plunged down. Both were stained oak. Photos occupied the walls, mom, dad, three teenagers - all boys. A hallway straight ahead of us ended at a swinging door to what was most likely the kitchen. No bedsprings creaked above us. No one called out to ask who was busting into their house in the middle of the night.

I motioned Brody inside.

Brody closed the door. He flipped the lock, then seemed to realize what he had done and looked over at me, sheepishly. *Habit,* his shrug seemed to say. "Okay," I said, speaking softly; it was eerie, how quiet it was inside the house. Moisture beaded on my upper lip, the back of my neck. The interior of the house was almost clammy. "We should do a room-by-room sweep, be sure we're the only things in here. Then we'll hit the kitchen and see what supplies there are. You with me?"

"Yes sir," Brody said. He almost didn't sound like he was mocking me.

We checked the second floor first. I left Brody guarding the stairwell as I crept bedroom to bedroom, shining the flashlight into corners, under beds, inside closets. The medicine cabinets had been emptied out. In the master bedroom, a gun case lay open and empty on a four-poster bed. Clothes were missing off of hangers; the sock and underwear drawers appeared to have been simply ripped out and tipped into suitcases. As I had suspected, these people had long since bugged out.

I tried not to wonder what must have happened to drive them from the safety of their houses.

Brody insisted on checking the basement. I didn't argue too hard against it; I had never been particularly fond of basements, and our discovery down in Peach Tree's fallout shelter had done nothing to make me more enamored of close, dark, underground spaces. I breathed a sigh of relief when Brody reemerged with the flashlight. "Anything?" I asked.

"Just a big-ass family room and a sweet home theater system," Brody said. "I wouldn't mind living here. Have you seen the dog?"

I hadn't. Brody frowned. Together, we looked down the hall. The door to the kitchen was still closed. Something about that seemed ominous. "Want to flip a coin to see who goes first?" Brody suggested, lightly.

"I'll go first," I said, automatically.

Brody glanced at me. His expression was hard to read in the dark. "That wasn't what I meant, Lieutenant," he said.

Just the same, I did go first, with Brody holding the flashlight over my shoulder, its beam trained on the swinging door. I concentrated on placing my boots soundlessly around any creaking boards. Could Brody actually hear my heart hammering, I wondered? Rifle against my shoulder, I eased the door open one-handed.

A beat passed. Then: "We're clear," I announced.

I heard Brody release the breath he had been holding.

The kitchen had a back door, with a doggie door cut into it. The window above the sink overlooked a backyard deck and barbecue pit. The cupboards were all standing open, but, to my relief, the family had left behind plenty that was edible: cans of fruit and vegetables; boxes of cereal and crackers; packages of juice drinks. Brody lay the flashlight down - its beam shone through an arched doorway into what looked like an elegant, teak-paneled dining room - and snatched something up off the counter. It was a full, unopened bag of Doritos. "Who heads off into the alien apocalypse and leaves behind Doritos?" he wondered, ripping open the bag. His expression, when he crunched into the first nacho-flavored chip, was exultant. I had to laugh.

"You and junk food, man," I said. "Ice cream for breakfast, candy bars for lunch, potato chips for supper...Is this how you eat all the time?"

Brody started to answer. About that time, the dog made a sound.

She was in the dining room. I turned around - the dining room was the one room we hadn't cleared, and I thought now how reckless that was, how inexcusable. What would Sergeant Donovan have said? This was not a fucking road trip with my pal from school. Letting my guard down even for a second could get the both of us killed. One thing my father had drilled into me was that an officer was responsible for the life of every soldier under his command.

I threw my arm out, blocking Brody's path to the doorway. Enough moonlight found its way into the kitchen for me to see his mouth turn down. "River - "

"It's Lieutenant," I said. "And you don't go anywhere until I give the order. Got it?" Brody nodded. "Good," I said. "Now back up, and cover me with that Beretta."

Looking none too pleased about it, Brody backed up.

I led into the dining room with my rifle. My gaze swept the corners. Shadows - all I could bloody well see were shadows. The windows were covered by long, lacey curtains that seemed to turn aside the moonlight, refracting what did make it through into star-shaped patterns; at the end of the long oak table, the dog was sitting in a pool of darkness. She whined when I came into view.

I knelt down cautiously, extending one hand toward her. Cold sweat trickled down my back. Without air conditioning, the house should have been stifling, yet the dining room was like a meat locker. "C'mon, girl," I murmured. "Come here. What's the matter, huh? What is it?"

The dog lay down with her chin on her paws. And that was when I saw it.

It was lying against the wall, on its side, shivering. I must have cried out; that proved too much for Brody, who burst around the corner holding the Beretta with both hands. "What is it?" he hissed, wildly.

"I - I think it's dying," I think I said.

The thing lying on the floor looked up at me. Its eyes were a wintry shade of grayish-blue. They reminded me of the time my father and I went hiking in the Himalayas, on one of his rare vacations. The horizon that high up had been a vista of purples, whites, and blues, the sky seeming to absorb the paleness of the snow. I remembered thinking back then about the stars. How they were still there, behind the lightness of the sky, even when we couldn't see them. Looking down at us as if from the other side of a one-way mirror.

Like the alien we had seen back on the Interstate, this creature's skin was purely white. Whereas the first alien had been eight or even nine feet tall, *this* one was barely four feet, if that. The outline of its ribs was clearly visible through its skin. Its chest rose and fell shallowly. Its knees were drawn up toward its stomach; its hands curled together against its breastbone, covering an ugly, black hole that had pierced straight through to its spine. Sticky silver liquid like mercury, only thinner, pooled on the hardwood floor around it. Like the substance we had seen back in Peach Tree's sheriff's station, I recalled. So it had been blood.

Alien blood.

I thought of the gun case open on the upstairs bed. Was this - this *thing* what had prompted the subdivision's residents to evacuate? Finding E.T. in your dining room would be enough to send most people into a panic...

"Jesus, it's just a kid," Brody said.

There was a muffled thud. He had dropped the Beretta on the floor as he knelt down next to me. He looked even paler and sweatier than he had in the kitchen, and I had been wondering then how much further he could stand to stumble on before daylight. "It's smaller," I agreed. "That doesn't mean it's younger. We don't know anything about their physiology."

"No," Brody said, with certainty. "It's a child. Maybe the other one we saw was looking for it. Maybe it was his dad, or something."

"Let's not anthropomorphize them," I said.

Brody looked at me with eyebrows raised. "River. Come on. They aren't *animals*."

Tell that to Sergeant Donovan, I couldn't help thinking. *Tell that to the people of Peach Tree. Tell that to the people who used to live in this house.* Bringing the flashlight around, I aimed the beam at the dining room's doorframe. A handprint was outlined there, in blood. Very red, very human blood. "Really?" I said dryly.

Brody flushed. Turning, he looked defiantly back at the dying alien-child, or whatever it was. "The dog isn't scared of it," he insisted. Like that proved something.

Indeed, the dog had wriggled forward until her nose was touching the creature's bald, domed skull. The tips of its fingers brushed her furry jaw. It had five fingers on each hand, five toes on each foot. Two eyes.

Two ears. A mouth. A nose. It was not exactly alien. But, it certainly wasn't human. The sentience studying me from beneath that protruding brow ridge was vastly, impenetrably Other.

I remembered something my mother had read to me once, from a Lovecraft story. *I felt myself on the edge of the world; peering over the rim into a fathomless chaos of eternal night.*

"It's cold." Abruptly, Brody rose. "I'm going to find it a blanket." He looked down at me, hard. "Don't do anything to it while I'm gone," he said.

I listened for his boots to thump up the stairs. Then I lay the rifle down, and drew the knife from my boot.

The creature looked at it. Its breaths were coming slower and slower, its eyelids beginning to fall toward its cheekbones. It had eyelashes, white and delicate as snowflakes. I wasn't really seeing it. I was seeing Donovan, on the quad, gripping my hand - looking at me across the vast expanse that separated life from death, and absolutely terrified. Beau Donovan had walked back to Scarcliff with two massive holes in his gut to warn the two of us about this alien and its friends. He had died trying to keep Brody and me safe. And this was one of the things that had killed him.

"What is it you want?" I asked, softly. "Why did you come here? What did any of us ever do to you?"

The thing parted its lips. It made a sound, very soft, like a sigh, or a whisper. *River -*

"River."

I jerked back. I had canted forward without realizing it, placing my ear just above the creature's mouth - my knife fallen forgotten to the floor.

It had said my name. Without speaking.

Brody was staring at me, stranded in the doorway clutching a blue comforter and a stack of clean, fluffy towels. I clambered up. My hands were shaking. The knees of my trousers were wet; I had unknowingly knelt in the creature's - the alien's - blood. I backed away in disgust. Something acidic burned against the backs of my eyes.

"River?" Brody said again, questioningly this time. I could not imagine what my face looked like. I marched out of the dining room, into the kitchen, braced both hands against the edge of the sink and stared into the moonlit yard.

More was dying inside that room than an alien. I could feel it. It was part of myself that was dying, the part that normally would have been sickened by the sight of any living creature's suffering. Brody still had that - compassion, empathy, mercy - and he had seen the same things today that I had.

The truth was, that part of me wasn't just dying. I was killing it. Deliberately. Holding back from walking into that room again, asking what I could do to help. I could *see* myself holding back, like I could see myself choosing not to do anything about it; and that, I thought, was the part of war no one could tell you about. You had to experience it for yourself to understand it.

You're too good for that.

I closed my eyes.

I was not unaware of Brody standing in the doorway behind me, twisting a silver-soaked towel in his hands. Nor was I unaware of the hush that had fallen over the dining room. I didn't say anything. Neither did Brody. When I opened my eyes again, there was only my own green-gray gaze staring back at me in the windowpane. The doorway was empty. Brody was gone.

By the time I finished with an icy shower in one of the upstairs bathrooms, he was back.

He was sitting on the double bed in what had to be a teenage boy's room. I had already rifled through the bureau for jeans, a clean pair of boxers, and a Metallica tee-shirt - the plainest, and smallest, shirt that I could find. I had dressed in the bathroom by the light of a citrus-and-sage candle. I had even shaved and brushed my teeth. I felt like a different person.

Fresh mud was splattered on the cuffs of Brody's trousers. He had tracked what looked like oil across the plush white carpet. Where he had been, I didn't bother asking. Sometimes, you just needed to be alone, to sort things out in your head.

I leaned back against the bedroom's built-in bookcases. Instead of books, they held CDs. "You okay?" I asked.

"I'm diabetic," Brody announced.

Having expected a slightly more existential response, I blinked. "I don't know what that means," I confessed.

"It means I need insulin." Brody took something out of his pocket. It was the slender black case I had seen him with back at Scarcliff. I had seen him with it on more than one occasion, over the three years we had been classmates. I had always assumed it was a fancy cell phone case - although cell phones were contraband for cadets, Brody had never seemed to think rules like that applied to him. He had always put it away the moment I saw him with it.

Now, I saw that inside was a pen-like instrument with a tiny needle at the tip, and a few vials of a clear, colorless solution. "I have enough left for about another day," Brody said. His voice sounded dull. "Then I'm out. Donovan was supposed to drive me into town to get some more after the holiday, but..."

But aliens had invaded, and the world, as Donovan himself would have said, had gone to hell in a hand basket.

I rubbed my temples. What felt like a stress headache was building behind them. "Is there some reason you didn't mention this little wrinkle until now, Private?"

"I thought I could pick up some more in Peach Tree. I didn't know we were going to find a fallout shelter full of bodies."

"And after I suggested setting out on a forty-three mile hike? You didn't think about mentioning it then?"

"I thought it was more like thirty-nine miles now."

I refused to crack a smile. I lowered my hands from my temples. "What happens if you don't get the insulin?"

"I'll slip into a coma," Brody said. "And then..."

Right. Diabetics couldn't live without insulin. I took a deep breath. "We'll just have to find a pharmacy," I said, with more confidence than I possessed. "There must be towns between here and Fort Green. Every town has a pharmacy. We can head back to the Interstate right now and get moving."

"On that note," said Brody, "I found something while I was out."

The "something" turned out to be two things: a pair of dirt bikes. Brody had rolled them up the split-level's front walk. I eyed them warily. "They aren't run by computers, like modern cars," Brody explained, kneeling by the one closest to the steps. Mud was caked into the treads of its tires. I stayed on the porch, slowly devouring a Power Bar. Off to the east, the sky was lightening to gray. "An EMP wouldn't have knocked them out. They needed gas, so I siphoned some out of the Navigator's tank - " I decided not to ask how a senator's kid knew how to do *that* " - and filled them up. They should run, but..."

"But?"

"They'll be noisy," Brody said. "And I'm not sure about your plan to stay hidden during the day. Driving after dark could be dangerous. We might break our necks running into the back of a stalled-out car we couldn't see."

He looked up at me expectantly, awaiting my decision. Because I was in command, whether I liked it or not.

Risks were inevitable in battle. From what I had read about them, I understood that. The trick was making the risks you took calculated ones.

The dirt bikes would reduce our journey to the fort from three or four days to possibly one. And Brody needed insulin, soon. We had a better chance of finding a town with a pharmacy before his medicine ran out if we were driving than if we were walking. It seemed the benefits, in this case, outweighed the risks of being spotted by our enemies. I popped the last bite of Power Bar between my lips. "You want to catch some rack time before we head out?"

Brody shook his head. "I'm good to go. Unless you need to sleep..."

"I'm fine," I said. When, in fact, my eyes felt like someone had poured sand in them, and every muscle in my body was aching from weariness. We had walked nearly twenty miles on almost no food in the past twenty-four hours, with only an hour of sleep between us back at that rest stop.

I didn't really want to sleep in the house with the dead alien, though.

That raised another issue. "Brody, you know we won't be able to take the dog with us, if we're taking the bikes," I said.

"I know." Brody kicked the bike's back tire glumly. There were crinkles at the corners of his eyes where his sunburn was starting to peel. "I don't think she would come, even if she could. She doesn't seem to want to leave the - the thing." The *child*, I knew he was thinking. It was true. The dog was still standing guard over the alien's corpse back in the dining room. She had growled at me for peering in at her earlier. Like she was daring me to move the body.

We dumped all of the dog food in the split-level's pantry into bowls for her, and I filled as many pots and pans as I could find with clean tap water, enough to last her for several days. While I packed a bag with more (human) food, some first-aid supplies, and fresh water for us, Brody showered and changed. He came down in jeans and a green V-necked tee-shirt. My borrowed clothes were too loose on me, the jeans rolled up twice at the cuffs. Brody's tee-shirt was just a little too tight. What must it be like, I wondered sourly, being a freakin' giant?

He had warned me the bikes would be loud. I still cringed when he fired the first one up. Had any birds been left in the trees, they would have taken off squawking. As it was, the leaves merely fluttered in the breeze, casting a net of shadows wide around us.

Brody swung his long legs over the larger dirt bike's seat. He was grinning. I climbed on my own, smaller bike. I had strapped my borrowed backpack on behind the seat using bungee cords. My camouflage cap was pulled down low over my ears, my rifle slung diagonally across my back. Brody smirked at me.

"You look pretty bad ass, Lieutenant," he shouted, over the bike's roar. "I may have to start calling you Rambo."

I called him a name that set him off laughing. As we pulled out of the split-level's drive, the sun was just cresting the horizon, spilling sorbet-colored light onto the rooftops.

****

I did not have much experience as a driver. I had only turned sixteen that April; I didn't even have a license, just a learner's permit. The bike was not the steadiest thing I had ever tried to steer, either. A couple of times, I was sure it was about to tip over. I kept a death grip on the handlebars.

Brody drove like a bat out of hell.

We screamed down the deserted Interstate at the bikes' top speed of fifty miles per hour, under the pinkish-orange light of the rising sun. Another ten miles past the subdivision, we had to slow down; all four lanes were slowly becoming clogged with stalled-out cars. No one was around, but there were signs that people had been through here, recently. Empty soda bottles had been pitched carelessly onto the asphalt, dirty diapers tossed into the ditches, suitcases abandoned on the shoulders. The detritus of a mass human exodus. I kept expecting to see a long column of survivors in the distance, trudging toward Fort Green like the Israelites fleeing from Pharaoh. But by midmorning, we had a little more than thirty miles behind us and had not come upon a living soul.

The first town we came to was nestled in a bend of the James River. Billboards along the Interstate directed us down an exit ramp toward gas stations, fast food joints, budget hotels - and a tourist-trap shopping center with, the billboard promised, a twenty-four-hour Walgreens Pharmacy.

The shopping center was one of those pretentious red brick affairs designed to make you feel like you were shopping on the commons of someplace sophisticated in New England. Landscaped walkways connected the various stores - Old Navy, Gap, Banana Republic, the ubiquitous Starbucks - around a central outdoor fountain. The fountain was no long plashing. On a normal July Fourth weekend, the courtyard would have been bursting with shoppers; every darkened window screamed at us with flyers advertising a GIANT INDEPENDENCE DAY SALES EVENT! Because there was nothing more American, I reflected, than buying cheap shit made in China.

Our dirt bikes sailed right through the empty parking lot. Brody cut his engine in the spot closest to the Walgreens' sliding glass doors. The pharmacy occupied a corner of the shopping center, the tallest building to either side by an entire story. I felt a sense of unease looking at it. Maybe it was because the automatic doors had been pried open.

Brody shot me a dirty look when I asked how he was feeling. "Look, man," he said, climbing off his bike. I was unfastening the bungee cords from my backpack and shrugging it onto my back. "I'm not any more breakable than I was before you knew I was diabetic, all right? So please stop looking at me like I'm about to collapse."

Touché, I thought.

Brody slid through the gap between the automatic doors ahead of me, turning sideways to fit. A wave of stale, stifling air hit us. I frowned down the long, shadowy aisles. Once again I had that feeling.

Someone was watching.

The interior of the pharmacy was filled with dim, smoky light. That light grew progressively lesser the further back the store extended; the back wall was completely swallowed in darkness. A row of checkout counters extended across the front of the store. The place was massive, a labyrinth of aisles selling cosmetics, greeting cards, and snacks. Brody drew his pistol. The shotgun was slung across his back, its barrel peeking over his shoulder.

We moved forward in sync, my flashlight sweeping the corners. I tried not to jump when the beam caught our reflections in the curved surveillance mirror above the cash register. "Where's the medicine?" I asked, in a whisper.

"It must be at the back." Brody nodded to the deepest pool of darkness. Wonderful, I thought. I indicated that I would take the lead. Brody followed on my heels.

As the pried-open doors had suggested, someone had been here before us: At the back of the store, the metal shutters over the pharmacist's counter had been broken open, the waist-high gate the pharmacist would stand behind to talk to customers kicked half off its hinges. Pill bottles were strewn across the tile behind the counter. "Tweakers," Brody said. "Aliens invade, and you've still got somebody whose first thought is stealing Oxy."

"Maybe they had a legitimate medical issue, like us," I protested.

Brody mumbled something. It sounded like *yeah, right.* "Stay here," he commanded. "I'll see if I can find the insulin."

I watched him go through the gate, bemused. So much for Brody taking orders.

I leaned back against the counter, keeping an eye on the store proper - as much of it as I could see in the dark. Brody rooted through cabinets behind me. I was trying to ignore the prickles of unease creeping across my scalp, the currents of air I could feel winding through the shadows.

I was trying not to think what would happen if the pharmacy didn't have any insulin.

Kyle Brody, diabetic. I wondered how many of the cadets at Scarcliff knew about his condition. I was willing to bet not many. Brody, dependent on a needle and some little vials of medicine to keep him going? It didn't fit with his devil-may-care image. Although, it made a certain kind of sense, knowing this about him. There was a lot about Kyle Brody and his cynical smartass shell that was starting to make sense, the more I got to know -

I straightened up suddenly.

Most likely, if I had not seen something like it on the road already, I never would have noticed the shimmer in the shadows - like the darkness had turned to water, and was rippling. But I had seen something like it, and without hesitation, I dropped the flashlight; swung my rifle up; aimed; and fired.

The shot was like a canon blast in the silence.

"Jesus-fuck!"

There was an almighty crash from the other side of the pharmacist's counter. A second later, Brody vaulted over it, ignoring the open gate. He skidded to a stop at the end of an aisle selling Band-Aids and antibiotic ointment. That was where I was, halfway down the aisle, kneeling over something.

"Christ," Brody whispered. "Did you shoot somebody?"

"Yes, Brody. I shot somebody." I glared at him. Did he think I would just open fire on some pathetic junkie? "No, I didn't shoot anybody. It's one of those things. One of those triangle drone-thingies. Like the one we saw on the Interstate."

Accompanied by a big-ass alien, I didn't add.

Brody light-footed down the aisle and knelt beside me, leaning on his shotgun. He had doffed his boonie hat somewhere. There was a white line around his forehead above where his sunburn began, showing where the hat had protected his skin. He reached out. His fingertips stopped just short of the silver triangle lying next to my boots. I heard him swallow.

"It's cold," he said.

I had noticed that, too. I did not know what thin-beaten material the object was made of, yet I was willing to bet it did not exist on this planet. I wasn't even sure whether it was metallic or organic; there was something much, much too alive about it. It was cold to the touch. Though my aim had been true, the bullet punching a hole right through the bottom of the triangle, there was still a slight vibration in it. There were no obvious circuits or switches or cameras, yet I was certain now this was the thing that had been watching us, probably sending back images of us to its alien masters.

I wondered if it was still transmitting. "Did you find your medicine?" I whispered. Brody nodded, patting his rucksack. "Good," I said. "Then I think we should get ou- "

We both heard the scraping sound.

My heart struck against my ribcage - a single, throbbing *gong* I tasted on the roof of my mouth. Brody's face had gone ashen beneath his sunburn. Pressing a finger to my lips - *not a sound* - I raised up slowly, just enough to see over the top of the aisle.

Something very large stood inside the sliding glass doors. Sunlight parted around it, seeming to glow on the hairless dome of its ivory-white skull.

I dropped back into a crouch. My stomach felt watery. *Back door,* I mouthed.

Brody nodded.

We crawled, Brody in the lead this time, careful not to bump anything or let our weapons clatter against the gate. I was supremely aware of the knife tucked down in my boot, of its cold, metallic edge resting against my ankle through my sock. I rounded the corner of the pharmacist's counter and pulled up short, motioning for Brody, who was about a yard ahead of me, to find some cover.

Something was moving down the Band-Aid aisle toward us.

I could neither hear nor see it, but I could feel it. It was how I imagined animals in the jungle felt, when a predator was stalking them unseen from the treetops. The hair on the backs of my arms was standing straight up. In the pit of my stomach was a knot so tight I thought I might throw up. I saw Brody duck behind one of the pharmacy shelves. Almost at the same time, an enormous figure loomed up on the other side of the counter.

I flattened my back against the wall. The rifle was clutched against my chest. The alien was standing right over me, separated from me by a couple pieces of plywood and a plastic countertop; all it had to do was look down, and it would see me. What would it do then? I couldn't even begin to imagine, but I felt my spine begin to burn, like it was already being ripped out through my back...

The figure retreated.

I went limp with relief. Could it be - *leaving*? Summoning all of my courage, I turned, and looked up at the counter.

There was nothing. No white face. No wintry pair of gray-blue eyes looking down at me.

The alien was gone.

Later, I would realize that made no sense. It had to know we were in the store. The drone thingy hadn't shot itself.

At the moment, however, all I could think about was getting the hell out of there. I crawled forward on my hands and knees, looking for Brody. I found him shortly, at the back of the store, crouched down beside the back door. It was just the littlest bit ajar.

Brody's eyes were blue as glass. "There's dozens of them out there," he said, softly. "*Dozens.*"

"Are you serious?"

Brody nodded. I sat back on my haunches, digging my fists into my eyes. *Fuuuuuck*, was what I was thinking. I was exhausted, I was hungry, and I was terrified, but I couldn't give in to the despair threatening to overwhelm me. There had to be a way out of this, if I could just keep it together and *think*.

Our bikes were parked out front. The aliens were out back. The engines would make noise, but what was the better option for escape: speed, or stealth? My brain said speed. Anything to get us out of there, and fast. But my gut said stealth. *The good Lord gave you instincts for a reason, Lieutenant Lane,* I imagined Donovan saying. *Use them.*

"Okay," I whispered, and quickly outlined my strategy.

It wasn't complicated. Brody listened raptly. When I finished, he nodded, and rose from his crouch. I rose as well. He had regained some color, I was pleased to see. Pacifist though he might have been, Kyle Brody was no coward. "Stay close to me," I commanded.

The shadows inside the store seemed denser now. Maybe it was just because I didn't dare use the flashlight. Maybe it was because the sun had gone behind a cloud outside. I held my breath as the front doors came into view, pushed wide open now. I saw nothing but parking lot on the other side -

Brody gasped. I heard it, and started to turn - but something grabbed me, something that gripped like iron. It was hands - cold, white, massive hands, wrapped tight around the tops of my arms. I bit back a cry of pain as I was lifted, slammed backwards against a shelf - the backpack strapped to me absorbed the brunt of it, but still, it hurt; I heard a clatter, saw bottles of shampoo and conditioner roll out into the aisle...

And still I was being lifted, higher, higher, my boots no longer touching the floor. My arms were breaking from the pressure of that massive grip, the bones connecting my shoulders to my elbows slowly being crushed; I kicked out, desperately, and received another painful shake as a reward. This time, my head cracked against the shelf. I bit my tongue, tasted blood behind my lips.

The creature holding me looked straight into my eyes. It had lifted me onto its level, a full three feet off the ground. Its face was too human, and too not-human at the same time; its gaze locked with mine, and something cold and piercing as a blade spiked through my forehead.

There can be no resistance.

The voice did not speak to me in words. Certainly it did not speak in English. Yet I understood it, like I understood the expression of the creature holding me suspended off the floor. It was remorseless. Relentless. It would never stop. It would never let us go. If we escaped, it would hunt for us until it found us.

Its eyes were the same color as those of the creature that had died back in that subdivision. Up close, they were like oceans, vast and limitless. Its skin was too smooth, white veins like fat worms threading just beneath the surface. And it was strong. So strong. I wasn't sure it even realized its grip was hurting me.

I could not see Brody. I didn't really need to. The thing had been lying in wait to ambush us; I was sure it had taken Brody out before grabbing me. That was basic battle strategy - take out the bigger guy first.

Size wasn't everything, though.

I twisted. It took all of my strength to do it, and still I thought my arms would be wrenched right out of socket; but the thing released me at the last second, and I fell hard to my knees, stifling a cry as pain lanced into my hip. My mouth tasted of salt and copper.

Gingerly, I curled my hands around my ankles, cowering against the shelf at the alien's white bare feet. Like I was trying to make myself as small and insignificant as possible. Between its tree trunk legs, I saw Brody lying in a heap, shotgun fallen out of his reach. His eyes were closed. I prayed he was just knocked out.

There can be no resistance, the thing had said. Yeah well, I thought. Screw that.

I yanked the hunting knife out of my boot and thrust it upward.

I put all of my strength behind it, not knowing how tough the alien's skin would prove; to my surprise, it parted like paper - like skin, I would think later; like the thin tissue that skin was. The alien made a sound, part gurgle. Its hands reached automatically for its stomach. I threw my weight against the blade, driving it deeper, twisting it - reaching up with my other hand as the alien bent double in pain, clamping my palm over the alien's mouth.

Gray-blue eyes bored into mine. I felt a pain in my wrist - the alien had grabbed my hand, the one holding the knife, and was twisting it. I yanked the blade free, and plunged it in again immediately, this time into the alien's neck.

Its eyes bulged. Hot, silver blood poured over my fingers, down the alien's hairless chest, onto the front of my shirt; we were locked in a silent, furious struggle, the alien's powerful hands scrabbling up, grappling me down onto the tile. Its weight bore down on me, pinning me to the floor as it slumped forward, writhing. Its hands tried to find purchase around my throat. Somehow I managed to hold onto the knife, forcing it deeper, deeper, smothering the alien's gurgling cries with my other hand all the while.

I wouldn't realize until later that I was crying.

It seemed an eternity before the creature finally shuddered and lay still. My hands were shaking. Unable to even free the knife, I wriggled out from under it. On my knees, cradling the wrist it had tried to snap, I stared at it.

It had to be more than nine feet tall, stretched out full length. A pool of mercury-like blood was widening around it, flowing toward the triangle-shaped object lying nearby. I could still feel the smoothness of its skin against mine. I shivered.

Then I thought, *Brody*.

When I reached him, he wasn't moving. For a panicked second, as I rolled him over, I thought -

"River?"

Brody's voice was thin and scratchy. I shushed him, gently. The silence inside the store was too heavy, the darkness to deep; I didn't know where the dead alien's buddies had gotten to, but I knew we could not afford to be here when they came looking for him.

On the third try, I managed to sling Brody's arm around my shoulders. I staggered to my feet with him leaning against me. The shotgun I had draped over my arm, along with my M16. The rucksack and backpack I hung around Brody's neck. Brody looked at me blearily. His scalp was gashed open above the ear, a scarlet stain spilling over his cheek and jaw, onto the collar of his tee-shirt. "I don't think..." His voice was thick. He swallowed. "I don't think I can walk, Lieutenant."

Anyone who knew my father probably would have recognized the stubborn line my jaw settled into at that. "Lean on me, Private," I said. "I'll get us out of here."

If there was a God, the only explanation I had for how we made it across that parking lot without being spotted was that He (or She) must have been watching over us. I didn't know what had become of the creatures Brody had seen behind the shopping center. I never turned around to see if we were being followed.

By the time we shuffled back up the exit ramp, I was dragging Brody. I stumbled across all four lanes; slid down the embankment on the far side; and deposited my much taller companion in the weeds. Brody mumbled incoherently. "It's all right," I kept saying, as I fumbled open the zipper on my backpack. "We're all right now."

I fished out the gauze and antiseptic I had lifted from the split-level's master bathroom. Brody winced when I dabbed at the gash above his ear. It really needed stitches, but I had no way to go about that, so I just said: "Brody. Hey. Brody." I glanced back up at the Interstate. The day had become still - airless. The humidity made it feel like we were breathing underwater. I couldn't stop my hands from shaking. "Stay awake, Private. Do you need your insulin?"

"Time is it?" Brody murmured. His eyes kept sliding in and out of focus.

"I don't know. Eleven-thirty, maybe?" I was gauging by the sun, something I wasn't very skilled at. I had no watch.

Brody shook his head. "I'm okay," he said, and closed his eyes again. I hoped he was with it enough to know what he was saying.

The back of my head was throbbing where it had been cracked against that shelf. I peeled off my tee-shirt - it was soaked with the alien's blood - and threw it into the weeds. I had had the foresight to pack us each a change of clothes back at the subdivision. I slipped on a clean tee-shirt now, and lay back in the grass next to Brody. The fingerprint-shaped bruises on my upper arms ached in time to my heartbeats.

What the hell were these things, and what the hell did they want?

Those were the questions I puzzled on as I watched clouds drift back and forth across the hazy midday sun. I was still musing on them an hour later when Brody stirred and sat up. He had lost his hat back at the pharmacy. He pushed his fingers through his spiky hair, biting his lip when they encountered the knot above his ear. There was dried blood on his cheek, which was swollen and starting to bruise. "What happened?" he groaned.

I filled him in on the alien ambush. Brody looked impressed. He was sitting cross-legged now, sipping from a bottle of water. I lay on my back, arms folded behind my head. "You just stabbed it?" Brody said.

Just. "Yeah," I said. "Why? What did you want me to do to it?"

"Nothing. I just thought they'd be more...you know. Indestructible."

"Let's be glad they're not," I said.

"They kind of look like us. Like humans." Brody was thoughtful. "Did you ever read about the Human Genome Project?"

What surprised me was that Brody had. "What about it?"

"Did you know scientists found these strings of DNA in humans that don't occur in any other organism on Earth? Apparently it's the part of our genetic code that's responsible for how our brains evolved to be so much more sophisticated than animals'. Some people say it's proof that God made man in His image. Other people say it's proof that aliens visited us, hundreds of millions of years ago, and spliced their DNA with ours. It's called the Prometheus Theory."

It sounded to me like a bunch of nutcases in the desert wearing tinfoil caps, hunting for messages in the stars. Then again, maybe those nutcases hadn't been so nutty after all. I sat up. Brody passed me the water bottle. "We had to leave the bikes," I told him.

Brody made a face. Though still pale, he did not seem as dazed. Hopefully his concussion would be a mild one. The upside of him being so hard-headed, I thought, and grinned into my water. "We can't be that far from Fort Green now, can we?"

"Ten miles, maybe?" I was guessing, but it was an educated guess. Not far off, I could hear the river babbling. I might not have been aware of it, had there been traffic whirring by, power lines humming overhead. Funny how quickly your ears adjusted to silence. "I bet that's why these things assembled here. They probably have a command post nearby, keeping an eye on the fort. Something to face off against our army, when it gets here."

"Or maybe they just wanted to beat the crowd to the Banana Republic sale," Brody quipped. I threw a blade of grass at him, which made him smirk. "Seriously, though, if we're that close, I say we get up and get going. We could be there before dark."

He was right, but - "Brody?"

"Yeah?"

"What are we going to do if we get there, and we don't find anybody?"

It was not a fear I wanted to voice out loud. Forty-eight hours ago, I would not have admitted to Kyle Brody that I was afraid of anything.

Brody turned his head, gazing up at the Interstate. A minivan was parked on the shoulder. It had a Baby On Board sticker in the back glass. "What would your father say we should do?"

I swallowed. I had been trying not to think much about my father. I was starting to suspect my theory about Washington, D.C., and its missile defense system was total crap. My father was most likely dead. "He would say we find a way to keep going. No matter what. He would say to survive and go on fighting, whatever it takes."

"I guess that's your answer, then." Brody turned back to me, smiling thinly. The sun over his shoulder hid most of his expression. For some reason, I was glad of that.

"I think we should stay off the road from here on out," I said.

****

The river was further away than I had thought. More like five miles, instead of two. The recent rains had turned the fields around the Interstate into swamps; the mud kept trying to suck off our boots. The only good thing I could say about being invaded by aliens was that they seemed to have destroyed all of the mosquitoes. Otherwise, we would have been eaten alive.

We reached the tree-shaded banks of the James River late on the airless afternoon of July Fifth. The temperature had topped out near one hundred degrees; the humidity was probably close to ninety percent. We both looked like we had been swimming. Our hair and clothes were drenched with sweat, our water bottles empty. One of the reasons I had decided to make for the river was that it would provide an endless supply of fresh water, without forcing us to venture into potentially overrun towns or subdivisions to resupply.

The other reason was that the James River bent around the northern edge of Fort Green. Following it rather than the Interstate, I was hoping we could reach the fort without another close encounter.

Brody had other ideas about what the river would be good for. Dropping his shotgun and rucksack in the rocks, he started tugging off his boots. "What are you doing?" I asked.

"What's it look like I'm doing?" Brody stripped his sweat-soaked shirt off, kicked out of his jeans and boxers. Grinning like a madman, he dove into the wide, foamy brown water with a whoop.

After a moment, I shucked out of my clothes and followed him.

The water was like heaven. I dove down as deep as I could - nowhere near the bottom. When I surfaced, someone splashed me. It was Brody, treading water and laughing. Sunlight dappled the surface of the water, woven with shadows from the trees that grew along the rock-strewn, marshy banks. Leaves and branches were carried past on the swift current. There were no sounds other than the water gurgling around us.

It was the first time since I had woken up at Scarcliff the day before that I hadn't been afraid.

Brody seemed to be feeling the same way. "What we need," he said, flipping onto his back, "is a cooler full of Bud Light, some music, and a bunch of girls in bikinis. The bikinis could even be optional."

I had to admit that sounded awesome. Not that I would ever have had the guts to go skinny-dipping with a bunch of girls.

That sounded scarier than fighting aliens.

I rolled over on my back as well, letting the current take me where it wanted. Every inch of me was bruised and weary. The cut over Brody's ear had stopped bleeding, but the bruise was spreading across his cheek, sending out feelers from a puffed-up center. "How are you feeling?" I asked.

Instead of answering, Brody said, "Do you think she's all right?"

Something tightened in my throat. I nodded. "I mean, we left her with her parents..."

Brody looked over at me, brow furrowed. "Huh?"

"I said we left her - " I stopped. Heat was creeping up my neck. I hoped, without much real confidence, that my sunburn might disguise it. "You were talking about the dog, weren't you?"

"Of course I was talking about the dog." Brody was beginning to sound amused. "Who were you talking about?"

There was nothing for it. "The girl from the rest stop," I confessed. "Cheyenne."

"I knew it!" Brody whooped again. I ground my teeth together. "You thought she was cute, didn't you?"

"Didn't you?" I said.

Brody waved that aside. "You should have gone for it, man."

"Okay."

My tone was sarcastic. Brody sat up, treading water. "Why not?" he asked.

"Because I don't think she was interested, all right?" I hoped my tone would convey that the subject should be dropped. Brody didn't seem to pick up on it.

"You'll never get anywhere with girls like that," he advised, sagely. "Girls like a guy with confidence."

Girls liked guys with blonde hair and blue eyes and washboard abs, in my experience. Having a rich senator daddy never hurt your chances, either. "Brody, we're in the middle of an invasion - "

"Exactly!" Brody said. "You gotta use this shit to your advantage, Lieutenant. You should have sung her that song. 'We got tonight; who needs tomorrow? Let's make it last, let's find a way' - "

I splashed him. Brody broke off, cackling, and splashed me back. I retaliated, and there ensued a splash war, of which I was confident I would have been the victor - I was smaller, faster, and I fought dirtier - if Brody hadn't dived forward to dunk me.

His hands stopped just short of my shoulders. He looked at me, water dripping off his nose, sparkling on the spiky tips of his hair. "Oh man," he said, softly. He was staring at the bruises on my arms. They had been covered by my tee-shirt before; only now did Brody seem to see how deep and black they were, circling my skinny biceps in the perfect shape of handprints. "Damn. That thing really tried to kill you, didn't it?"

There can be no resistance. "I'm pretty sure it meant to kill us both," I said. Brody touched the gash above his ear unconsciously. He had gone pale again. The day seemed quieter now that we weren't trying to drown one another. Shadows had begun to gather under the trees. I consoled myself that it was just because the sun was beginning to dip down in the west. I nonetheless wished for a breeze, something to stir them - something to prove they were only shadows. "Brody. Listen. Back...back at that gas station, outside of Peach Tree. While you were in the bathroom - "

"You stole a hat." Brody's smile was more wan than usual, but he managed one. "I know. I've seen you wearing it. God will forgive - "

"No. Listen to me." I had not meant to tell Brody this, but now that I had started, I just wanted to get it over with. "I saw something. I think it was Donovan."

Brody went still. There was something stark behind his eyes. Something that made him look younger. "Donovan," he repeated, slowly. "Sergeant Donovan."

I nodded. "Yes. Sergeant Donovan."

"You saw Sergeant Donovan. At the gas station." Brody was speaking slowly, like he was processing the words as he was saying them. "After we watched him die. After his body disappeared off the quad."

"Yes."

"You *saw* him?"

"Yes, Brody, listen." I sighed, pulling Brody out of the path of a log that was bobbing toward us; the river was full of little swells that made it difficult to see very far up or down it. On the opposite shore, golden afternoon light bathed the trees in a rich summer glow, but I was starting to feel cold. "I was looking in the mirror above the hat stand. I saw him walk up to the window and look in at me. When I turned around, there was nothing there." I shuddered, just remembering.

Brody, inexplicably, smiled. "River. Come on. We had just been through something awful. Probably you imagined - "

"Brody," I said.

Brody waved me off. "Just hear me out. Probably you imagined - "

"*Brody*." I squeezed his wrist tightly. The bones in my body seemed to be crumbling away to ash; I was surprised I had the strength to keep swimming. "Brody. *Bodies*."

I could tell Brody didn't want to look. But he did.

It was not a log floating past us. It was a man. He had dark skin; as he was floating face-down, that was all I could really see about him, except that he was wearing a business suit. A massive hole had been punched through the center of his back. Just like the holes that had been punched through Sergeant Donovan.

More bodies floated behind that one. Dozens of them. Dozens and *dozens*. They were men and women from all walks of life - I saw suits, dresses, blue jeans, a clerical collar, police uniforms, medical scrubs, coveralls - of all races and ages, every barrier that could be thought of to separate the living - race, class, gender, religion - meaningless in death. One little girl was bobbing along face-up. The wet curtain of her hair brushed the cheek of a wrinkle-skinned old man. Bile started to burn in the back of my throat.

Then, we heard the screams.

They were distant, a mile or so to the east, accompanied by another sound that seemed to quick-start my frozen heart.

Gunfire.

I do not know who made it to the bank first, me or Brody. I was the first to yank my jeans back on - "Bring your medicine," I shouted, pointing toward Brody's rucksack. Brody was cursing, hopping around on one foot trying to drag his jeans up over his wet hips. I grabbed the rifle, leaving my shirt and boots on the bank, and tore off into the trees.

The ground was littered with sticks and stones. Later, I would find bruises where the stones had pierced my feet. I did not feel them at the time. The river was turning, and I turned with it, trying not to look at all those poor dead people choking the water we had just been swimming in; then, suddenly, I had burst out from behind the trees, the sun was shining in my eyes, and something was towering over me.

It was a bridge, packed with screaming, panicked people. It was from there more bodies were falling.

I dropped to one knee in the mud, rifle aimed up the incline at the bridge. Cars, vans, and semis were stalled all along it, on the four lanes of the Interstate leading up to and across it; I could hear what breeze there was whistling through the arched iron girders, that sound somehow even louder than the hysterical screams of the fleeing people and the rat-tat-tat of gunfire from the far side of the bridge.

An enormous white shape loomed up behind a teenage girl. She was running toward an overturned school bus, seeking cover. She was not going to make it. The breath went still in my lungs.

I pulled the trigger.

The alien stumbled. I barely heard the crack of the M16; barely felt the kickback against my bruised shoulder. The girl dove behind the bus. I would remember later how she looked at me, maybe the first time a girl had ever looked at me and seemed to *see* me; but already I was up and running, running straight past her, flashing up the incline onto the bridge.

Along the way, Brody fell in beside me.

A bullet-ridden Mustang blocked our path. I skirted it; Brody slid across the hood. The alien I had shot turned toward us. Silver blood dripped out of a perfect, round hole in the center of its massive chest. I felt the force of its icy gray gaze slam into me, as one of its giant arms came up; it was holding something in its hand, something with a long, silver barrel that was glowing blue; the hairs on the backs of my arms stood up -

Brody shot it.

I did hear the shotgun blast. It practically shattered my eardrum. I turned. Brody, in jeans and nothing else, never missed a beat. "Keep moving!" he shouted, at the thirty or so people still sprinting toward the bridge. More of the alien creatures were marching up the Interstate behind them, seemingly in no hurry. Because I knew what to look for now, I could see the shimmers of air that bespoke the triangle-shaped objects floating to either side of them. They were marching in formation, in perfect synchronicity - a triple column of enormous, white-skinned, icy-eyed alien soldiers. There must have been three hundred of them.

"Lieutenant! Come on!" Brody grabbed me by the waist. I let myself be hauled backwards onto the bridge, Brody all but carrying me. That strange, disconnected sort of calm began to settle over me again. I looked left and right, saw people crouched behind cars, frozen with terror, aliens lying in pools of silver blood, one of the triangle-shaped objects whirring pathetically on the asphalt, like a bird with its wing sheared off. Black fluid leaked from a crack in its silvery shell.

"We have to get these people off the bridge," I said, calmly.

Brody glanced at me, then nodded. He slung his shotgun over his shoulder and drew the Beretta from his waistband. The alien he had shot was lying on its side, a smoking, fist-sized crater where its nose should have been. I could see the whitish bones of its skull, the unmistakable gray matter of brain tissue inside the wound. "I'll cover you," Brody said. I nodded.

At the far end of the bridge, sunlight glinted off of metal. The sky on that side of the river was smeared with clouds too thick to be anything but smoke. I did not allow myself to think through the implications of that yet. I darted barefoot between the cars, thinking how wild I must have looked - a skinny, dark-haired, sunburned teenage boy in loose jeans and no shirt, toting an M16 like I knew how to use it. Which, fortunately, I did. "Come on," I encouraged, beckoning people to their feet, hauling them up physically when they seemed too frozen to move on their own. "Come on. You can't stay here. You have to keep moving. Keep moving!"

To my surprise, every single person did as they were told.

When the last person - the girl I had saved, as it so happened - was safely away, I turned. Brody had taken cover behind a Jeep. The alien army continued its relentless march onto the bridge. "Brody!" I shouted. "Come on!"

Brody jumped up, firing off a few rounds for good measure, and started running.

The aliens opened fire.

They were all holding those strange, long-barreled weapons. I felt the sizzle of something, a round that felt more like a tongue of flame than a bullet, shave the skin above my hipbone. I cried out. Brody staggered into me - for a second, I thought he was falling. Then I realized *I* was the one who was falling; my right leg seemed to have given out. Brody gripped me under the arms, keeping me on my feet. "Move!" I heard a voice I didn't recognize shouting at us; and somehow, Brody had an arm around my waist, and while the air around us turned to smoke and electricity from whatever the aliens were shooting at us, we managed to keep running.

The end of the bridge was mere feet in front of us. A line of overturned cars spread across it. A barricade. That was the metal I had seen glinting in the sunlight. Men and women in camouflage fatigues fanned out behind it, armed with a hodgepodge of rifles, shotguns, pistols, and grenades. They were the most beautiful sight I had ever seen.

A slender young black man in fatigues darted out to us. I half fell into him. My side was on fire. Something sticky was running down the inside of my pant leg. "Now!" I heard the young soldier yell. "Blow it now!"

A rumbling noise filled my ears. The ground beneath our feet seemed to pitch, then buckle. I fell, Brody fell, the soldier fell, all in a heap just behind the barricade; behind us, although I was already unconscious by then and didn't see it, a fireball plumed into the cloudless sky, and the bridge collapsed into the water.

*****

"Put him down over there, Marco. Over there."

I moaned. I was being lowered, gingerly, onto a rough, wooden surface. "Brody," I heard myself gasp, automatically.

"Is that the name of your buddy?" someone asked.

I opened my eyes. The slender black soldier was looking down at me.

We were in what looked like the gymnasium of an elementary school. I had been placed on top of a wooden door lain across two metal trashcans to form an exam table, like in a doctor's office. A woman with gray hair tied up in a bun and a stethoscope draped around her neck was ordering soldiers around, though she herself was in civilian clothes. Most of the wounded were either sitting up pressing rags over their cuts and gashes, or lying down on the bleachers with IVs snaking into their arms. I did not see Brody anywhere. My pulse skittered sideways in my throat. "Kyle Brody," I said, firmly. "We're classmates. He's - "

"He's right over there. Getting seen to by Corporal Owens." The soldier pointed. I relaxed. There was Brody, standing by a folding table covered with bandages, underneath one of the basketball goals. A dark-haired female soldier wearing a pair of latex gloves was daubing at the hours'-old cut above his ear. Other than that, he appeared unharmed.

My side was still burning. I looked down at it. "It's not too bad," the soldier assured me, sympathetically. It seemed to me that he was right: My hip looked more burned than blasted, blisters crawling up the tanned skin across my ribs. I had been afraid half of my side would be missing. I had seen what the aliens' weapons could do to the human body.

The soldier leaned back against the makeshift exam table. He had a bruise on his cheek, a white bandage around one wrist. The wounds did not look fresh. "Looks like you boys were out in the shit," he remarked.

I explained that we were from Scarcliff Military Academy; told him about Donovan and the town of Peach Tree and the deserted subdivision; and ended with the alien I had killed inside the Walgreens. By then, the gray-haired doctor had made her way over to me. "Lie on your side," she commanded. I rolled onto my side, trying not to wince as her gloved hands probed my hip.

"We left some people," I said. "Back at this rest stop, near Peach Tree - "

"That's a long way from here, cadet. We've been sending out search parties, hunting for these alien bastards, bringing what survivors we could find back, but - well, you saw," the soldier said. "We had to blow the bridge. Won't nobody be going back across that now. Nor anybody, or anything, crossing over here, unless they can swim."

I nodded. I did not trust myself to talk.

You boys be careful, Cheyenne's father had said.

"All right." The doctor spoke brusquely. She was smearing something cold, like jelly, over the burn on my hip. I clamped my teeth together as she taped a moistened bandage over it. "You're lucky it's just a flesh wound. Nothing to worry about." That depended, I thought, on whether it was *your* flesh that had been wounded. "I'll have Corporal Owens bring over a shot of penicillin for you. Keep the burn clean and dry for the next few days, and it should heal up just fine."

She patted my arm. I assumed that was her equivalent of offering me a lollipop. I glared at her bun as she moved off.

The soldier was grinning like he knew what I was thinking. "Got a real bedside manner, doesn't she? I'd like to see one of those aliens give her any shit. She'd ram a tongue depressor up its - "

"Marco!"

The soldier spun around, instantly at attention. "Yes sir!"

A soldier with a salt-and-pepper buzz cut stood in front of the gym's outer door. A square of late afternoon sky was visible behind him. I had never seen the man before, but I recognized his rank by the colonel's bars on his jacket. "Briefing at sixteen-hundred hours, Sergeant," the colonel said, smartly.

"Yes sir." The soldier, Sergeant Marco, saluted. The colonel went out.

I sat up carefully. Thanks to whatever the doctor had smeared on it, my side was not burning beneath its bandage. I felt like I should give the table up to someone who really needed it, but at the moment, no one seemed to. "Are you all from Fort Green?" I asked, looking at the fifty or so soldiers milling around the gym.

"What's left of us." Sergeant Marco's tone was deceptively light. "I'm Isaac de Marco, by the way. Everybody just calls me Marco."

"River Lane." My tone was distant. I was trying to fathom less than a hundred men and women being all that was left of the twenty-five thousand soldiers stationed at Fort Green. It was one of the largest bases in Virginia. "The president - "

"He's here," Marco said. "He was at Fort Green when it happened."

The president was here? This was bad, I thought. He should have been rushed out of here on Air Force One a long time ago. "What did happen?" I asked.

"They bombed the hell out of us." Marco spoke matter-of-factly, arms folded across his chest. "It was the middle of the night. I was asleep in the barracks, with the other enlisted guys. We heard the air raid sirens go off, and then - boom." He made a starburst motion with his hands. I stared at them, at Marco's long, artistic fingers, hanging on every word. "Lights went out. People were running around, screaming. We could hear explosions, but no buildings were falling down, there weren't any fires burning - just heat. You could feel it, through the walls. Like we were inside a giant oven. The people we found later, mostly over by the family housing units, they were just cooked. I'm talking *char*-broiled. Me and some other guys, we started down to the fallout shelter, but Colonel Hall - " he glanced toward the door the man with the colonel's bars had just gone out " - came upon us, and told us to get the hell out. He said they were using some kind of neutron bomb, and on top of that, some kind of poison gas. Fallout shelters weren't going to protect us from that. Those of us that could, we made it out to the woods. Then we watched the motherfuckers land their ships right on the other side of the river and set up camp - after they sent some ships over to start collecting bodies," he added.

I sat up like I had been stuck. "Bodies?"

Grimly, Marco nodded. "Yeah. Don't know what they wanted 'em for, but after we realized what they were doing, some of us snuck back onto the base. This was late yesterday, after the gas had had time to disperse. We stole what weapons we could find, grabbed some C-4 to wire up that bridge, and set fire to the whole place. There wasn't time to bury the dead like we should have. But we couldn't let those bastards have them for science projects, or whatever."

There was no way, I thought, this could get any more sickening. "And the people on the bridge?" I asked. "Where did they come from?"

"All over." Marco shrugged. "We've been sending out scouts, like I told you. Our orders were to assemble at the bridge with any survivors we had found. We had those people halfway across when they attacked us." He shook his head in disbelief. "I swear to you, it's like they can come out of nowhere. We hadn't seen any of them since they attacked the base. Then all of a sudden, there they were. By the hundreds."

I thought of the enemy soldiers Brody had seen outside the shopping center, less than twenty miles up the Interstate. Had they been gathered there to plan their assault on the military's remaining defenses? Brody had said there were *dozens*, not *hundreds*. Had the others been hiding somewhere else, waiting for their shadowy drone devices to report back on the location of the soldiers that were trying to lead innocent people to safety? "Do you know...how much of the rest of the country is left?"

Marco shook his head. He didn't seem much older than I was. Twenty-five, perhaps. "I know we haven't had any contact, from anybody. None of our radios or cell phones are working. But you would have thought, if anyone was still out there, they would have sent some planes, or tanks, or something. I mean, we have the goddamn presid- Ah." Marco broke off suddenly. His voice had grown warmer. "Here's Corporal Owens. Gonna give the kid his medicine, Corporal?"

The dark-haired soldier I had seen tending Brody pursed her lips at Marco. He grinned, rubbing a hand through his hair in a self-conscious fashion. I had seen that move from other guys a thousand times, when they leaned up against their lockers to talk to a pretty girl. Even when the world was ending, I thought, some things never changed. "Left arm or right?" Corporal Owens asked me, holding up her syringe.

I chose the left. Owens stabbed the needle in above my bruises, then moved on to her next patient.

Brody had come sauntering over. He was now wearing a New York Yankees tee-shirt and a pair of flip-flops. He threw a shirt at me. It had a monkey eating a banana screen-printed on the front, and was nothing I would ever have chosen to wear myself. "Where did you get this?" I asked, suspiciously. Picturing Brody pillaging from the dead behind the gym...

"There's a stack of clothes and stuff out in the hallway," Brody said. "I would have gotten you some shoes," he glanced at my bruised, muddy feet, "but I didn't know what size you wore."

"We raided the stores in town this morning," Marco explained. "Gathered what we could, from what was left."

His tone said that had not been much. I had lived on enough military bases to know what this town would have been like, before the invasion. Towns always sprang up around bases, like mushrooms, feeding off the military families stationed there. I tried not to think about the children, both on the base and off, who had sat through assemblies in this gym, played basketball on this court. Most of them were probably dead now. "Does anyone have any clue what these things came here for?" I asked, forcing the brand-new shirt down over my head. It still had the tags on the bottom. I wondered if there was any chance of finding a new toothbrush around here.

Marco was checking his wristwatch. It was analog - still ticking. That stuck in my brain, buzzing around with a fuzzy idea that would not crystallize for me for a while yet. "I heard some crazy preacher-man going on about the Book of Revelations yesterday. Talking about 'the End Times,' and all that. Dr. Jordan said that's nonsense. She's got some theory about 'genetic bridges' and 'prehistoric extraterrestrial visitations' -"

"Like the ancient astronaut stuff?" Brody sounded intrigued. I recalled him going off about the Prometheus Theory and the Human Genome Project - aliens uploading us with their super-advanced DNA so we could out-evolve the animals, or whatever. I hoped this was not the same Dr. Jordan who had just examined me, and if there was some less, you know, bat-shit crazy person around who could give me a second opinion. "Like the aliens that supposedly built the pyramids and taught human beings how to speak and make fire, and stuff?"

"I guess." Marco's tone was noncommittal.

Brody noticed. "What do you think they want?" he asked.

His tone was challenging. Quite different from the way I had spoken to the sergeant. Marco looked between the two of us and grinned, like he understood something about us we didn't understand ourselves. "I think they're well-coordinated sons of bitches," he said, evenly, "and it's about time we got organized and sent them back to Mars or Saturn or Uranus, or wherever the fuck they came from. Now, if you'll excuse me, fellas," he straightened up, "I've got a briefing to attend."

I saluted before he walked off. It was only partly out of habit. I liked Sergeant de Marco. I was glad someone like him was fighting for our side.

Brody hopped up on the makeshift exam table next to me and started swinging his feet. I gave him a look. "What are you so happy about?"

"Two things," Brody said. "First of all, we made it. We're at Fort Green, and we're alive. I've got to hand it to you, Lieutenant. You made the right call in bringing us here. Secondly," he said, "I brought you something, since you dropped it when you passed out back there on the bridge."

He held up my rifle. *Donovan's* rifle.

I was sure Brody understood the distinction.

I took it him from gingerly. Brody was still smirking. I wasn't very good at saying thank you, especially not to Kyle Brody. I decided to go with something else. "Want to crash a top-secret military briefing with me, Private?"

Brody clapped me on the back. "I thought you'd never ask."

The briefing was held in the school's second-floor library. "Top-secret" proved to be an exaggeration; no one was guarding the doors, and Brody and I weren't even the only civilians in attendance, although we were the youngest by roughly a decade. Other than Sergeant de Marco, who grinned and nudged Corporal Owens in the ribs when he saw us, none of the forty or so adults in the room seemed to take any notice of us.

This included the president. *Of the United States.*

To a person, those assembled looked bedraggled. Colonel Hall stood behind a podium that looked like it had been carted in from one of the classrooms. A map of Virginia was tacked up on the wall. Tables and chairs had been pushed together in front of the lectern. Two men in dark suits whom I assumed had to be Secret Service agents were seated one on either side of the president. It was darkly comical, seeing such burly guys wedged into chairs made for third-graders.

Brody and I leaned against a bookshelf, next to a poster of Alice reading to the Mad Hatter.

"Here's what we know." Colonel Hall's gravelly voice quieted the murmurs among the crowd. "The enemy has forces established across the James River here, near the I-95." He tapped a wooden ruler against the map. Red push pins dotted it, marking the known locations of the aliens. There were, I was not thrilled to see, a lot of push pins. "Our reconnaissance squads have reported large concentrations of the enemy near Charlottesville and Richmond. The squad we sent north toward D.C. has not reported back - " everyone in the room glanced at the president, who was sitting with his back to me and Brody " - so we have no way of knowing whether or not they made it through. The fact that we have seen no support from the Pentagon, despite the Joint Chiefs knowing our president was here at Fort Green when we were attacked, suggests that our central command may have been disabled, as well."

He was talking about the Pentagon. Where my father worked. I looked straight ahead, avoiding Brody's gaze.

"We also know," Hall was saying, "thanks to reports from the survivors we found along the Interstate, that the blackout we're experiencing here extends in all directions for at least fifty miles. We have had numerous reports of gas attacks on civilian targets. We estimate casualties in Virginia to be in the tens of thousands. The strategy, in Virginia at least, seems to have been to cripple our military response capabilities using an EMP, or electromagnetic pulse," Hall was clearly dumbing this down for the civilian members of the audience, "while at the same time neutralizing our defense personnel using a neutron-style weapon. After that, the enemy began inflicting casualties on large civilian population centers using chemical agents. We assume the agent is a nerve gas of some type. However, since no bodies have yet been recovered, we cannot say for certain."

"Sir?" A soldier with a bloody bandage wound around his forehead spoke up tentatively from the corner. "Sir, what about radiation? People have been asking whether it's safe to stay this close to the fort, after it was bombed..."

"Thus far, our Geiger counter readings are normal, and none of the survivors from the fort have shown any signs of radiation sickness. That includes myself. The fact is," Hall braced his elbows on the podium, "we don't know what type of weapon was used against Fort Green. It does not appear to have been nuclear. Yet it was, obviously, extremely deadly."

The president sat back in his seat. He looked much the same as he did on TV - slight, fair-haired, with wire-framed glasses. Only now he was disheveled, wearing a wrinkled pinstripe suit. "You mentioned the bodies, Colonel. Do we, uh," the president cleared his throat, "do we know what these - *things* are doing, with the bodies?"

Hall's gaze jumped, almost imperceptibly, to Marco. "We have had scattered reports," Hall said, "of people known to have been killed in the attacks later being sighted among the enemy. At this time, those reports have been unconfirmed."

A few of the soldiers looked at one another in astonishment. The president had blanched. "Alive? You're saying they've been sighted *alive*?"

The way he said it made me remember that the president also had a wife, and children. I wondered where they were now.

I wondered if even the president knew.

"As I said, Mr. President, these reports have been unconfirmed." Hall's tone was stern. He nodded at Marco. "Yes, Sergeant?"

"Has there been any communication from the enemy, sir?"

"No, there has not. Not to our people, anyway. If the enemy has demands, he is not directing them to us." The colonel paused, looking gravely around at the gathered faces. The president had his hand over his mouth. The gray-haired doctor, Dr. Jordan, stood across the room. Her eyes were on the colonel, sharp as pins. As though she knew he was holding back more than he was saying. "At this point," Hall said, "we have to operate under the assumption that help will not be arriving. We cannot know if these attacks have been carried out farther to our north or our West. We cannot know what the situation is for our allies in Europe, Asia,

South America, or the Pacific. But even if the rest of the world has been untouched by this invasion, Mr. President, my officers and I agree that we can have no expectation anyone is even aware of our survival. We have no way to call for aid, and no way to know if aid is on its way. We must proceed as though it is not.

"The enemy, meanwhile, knows exactly where we are. They proved that this afternoon when they tried to take that bridge. And where we are, sir, is not a defensible position. My advice to you is that we find somewhere that is, and we dig in. Probably for the duration."

"Where do you think that would be?" Brody asked.

I jumped. It had been my idea to bring Brody to this briefing - but the last thing I had expected was for him to *talk* during it. I resisted the urge to scoot away from him. Hall, like everyone else in the room, was looking at us. The colonel had dark eyes and bushy eyebrows. It was a little bit like being stared down by a vulture. "And you are, son?" he asked.

"Someone who thinks trying to find a location to 'dig in' is pretty pointless," Brody said, "when these things have proven they can wipe out a military base in about five minutes."

A murmur ran through the room at that. Dr. Jordan looked amused. The president was looking at Brody with a faint line between his eyebrows, like he recognized him. It was possible he did. Brody's dad was a senator.

Hall tapped his ruler on the podium, calling everyone back to order. His expression was severe, yet what I noticed most about him right then were the lines of exhaustion scored deeply into his cheeks. "The enemy has had the element of surprise up until now. If we stay hidden - "

"But how are you going to do that?" Brody persisted. Hall started to say something; the president held up a hand, indicating that Brody should be allowed to continue. "Colonel, these things know everything there is to know about us. Where our military bases are. Where these large population centers are. Even where our president was going to be, the night before last. Do you think there is any move you can make they won't be aware of, won't already have anticipated?"

Hall glared at us. Though I hadn't said a word, it seemed I was guilty by association. "Do you have a suggestion for how else we might go about surviving, son, or did you just feel like pointing out the obvious?"

"We should talk to them," Brody said, at once. "We should ask for a parley. Try to find out what it is they want."

"I think they've made it clear what they want," Hall growled.

"Not all of them." There was something in Brody's tone I hadn't picked up on earlier. I realized now I should have. Brody was *excited.* Like he knew something I didn't know, something that had made him so eager to crash this briefing. Inexplicably, I felt betrayed. "I talked to some people downstairs. Other survivors. They said they saw an alien protecting a group of civilians - "

"Hostages." A woman wearing a captain's bars spoke sharply, rising from her seat. "I spoke with these same witnesses, Colonel. What they described was an enemy soldier, smaller than those that seem to be their primary combatants, leading a group of unarmed civilians away from a firefight. I think it's safe to assume they were not 'protecting' them. They were taking them as prisoners." She looked ruefully at Brody, like she pitied his naïveté. Brody glared at her.

I hoped he wasn't going to bring up the dog and the dying alien in front of the president.

"We need scouts," said Hall, before Brody could say anything. "The majority of our force will remain with the president and the civilians. We have more than two hundred souls under our protection now - women, children, wounded, and the elderly. I have spoken with my officers. We believe the best course of action is to move inland, toward the mountains, following the Interstates as much as possible - that will be our best chance of being found, if our allies are looking for us." It would also be really convenient for the aliens when they came to wipe out this two-hundred-plus group of women, children, wounded, and the elderly, but now did not seem like a good time to say that. "Because we cannot afford to walk into another ambush, we need volunteers to take the few ATVs at our disposal and scout the route ahead of us. The first group will pull out at zero-three-hundred hours, in advance of the main column, which will be leaving at dawn - with your permission, Mr. President." Hall added that almost as an afterthought. The president nodded, confirming my assumption that not much about this "briefing" had been news to him; this was the post-apocalyptic version of a press conference, to let the rest of us know what the people in power had already decided. "Dr. Jordan, if I could speak with you about readying the civilians..."

The briefing broke up then, chairs scraping back as people grouped together and started talking. The Secret Service agents rushed the president out of the library. Dr. Jordan made her way over to the colonel.

I turned to Brody. "I need to speak with Sergeant de Marco," I said.

"Whatever." Brody's tone was sour. "I'm going to find something real to eat. I hear there's an actual cafeteria, and honest-to-goodness sleeping bags to sack out on." He pushed off from the bookshelf. "Come find me, when you're finished?"

I promised that I would.

****

There was a cafeteria, although the food turned out to be just PBJs and cups of applesauce, washed down with cans of warm soda. The windows had been opened, allowing in a welcome nighttime breeze; Brody was nowhere to be found among the tables, but Corporal Owens told me she had seen him grab a pair of sleeping bags and head upstairs to the classrooms, where the civilians were being housed.

As Hall had said, there were more than two hundred of us. Some had survived the attack on the town or the base. Some had been stranded on the Interstate, rounded up by the soldiers Hall had sent out on recon. A few, like me and Brody, had headed to Fort Green under their own power, hoping to find help here. I said hello to the soldiers standing guard at the top of the stairs and picked my way around the slumbering civilians in the school's tiled upstairs hallway.

It was inside one of the darkened classrooms that I discovered Brody, sitting on a sleeping bag, talking to a girl.

Typical.

The girl was a plump redhead, dressed in cotton shorts and a Florida State tee-shirt. Only when she looked up at me did I realize she was the girl whose life I had saved on the bridge. I felt myself turn an extremely unbecoming shade of red.

"Hi," the girl said, shyly.

"Hey," I said. My throat was very dry, all of a sudden.

Brody, who of course had to be smirking, made the introductions: "River Lane, this is Alice Bachman. Alice, this is River. Alice wanted to say thank you, Lieutenant. I told her you'd be along eventually." He stood, dusting off his jeans. "I'll give you two a minute, shall I?"

He sounded absurdly pleased with himself.

I thought about shooting him.

Brody went out. I propped my rifle against the teacher's desk, laid my backpack down beside it. Twilight had fallen softly over the little riverfront town. The window above Alice's head was a dark mirror, showing me my reflection; I sat down quickly, on the sleeping bag beside her. Shadows observed us, pooled thickly around the desks someone had shoved into a corner. With Brody gone, it was just the two of us in the room.

"I saw you get shot earlier," Alice said.

I touched the bandage on my side through my tee-shirt. "It's just a flesh wound," I was quick to say.

"That was really brave, what you did," said Alice. "Running out onto the bridge like that, I mean." She glanced at my rifle. "Brody said you go to military school?"

"A military *academy*," I stressed, so she didn't get the idea Scarcliff was some reform school for degenerates, or anything. It was one of the most renowned military academies in the nation. Scarcliff's graduates went on to the Ivy League, to careers in politics, business, finance - and yes, the military, sometimes.

It suddenly occurred to me that asking about my school might really have been Alice's way of asking how old I was. I said, "I'm a junior. What about you? Are you in college?"

I nodded at her Florida State tee-shirt. Alice said, "I'll be a freshman, in August. I just graduated from high school in May."

"What are you studying? Or - I mean - what will you be?" *What would you have been,* I had almost said.

"Creative writing. Poetry. I know." Alice smiled, wryly, at my expression. "My parents had the same reaction. They made me promise to minor in 'something useful,' like business."

"Where are they now?"

I was almost afraid to ask, but Alice said, "On a cruise to Tahiti. It's like their second honeymoon, which is just so gross, I can't even..." She made a face. I laughed - glad that in the dark, she hadn't seen me blush even deeper at the word *honeymoon*.

Our backs were against the wall, Alice's shoulder almost touching mine, her knees drawn up and circled with her arms. Her white sandals were caked with mud. Her toenails, endearingly, were still painted robin's egg blue. "I was so excited to spend a week home by myself, you know? I had a movie in and was watching it with all the lights off when the power went out."

"Did you...see any of them?" I asked.

"Yes." Alice stared across the classroom like she was seeing something else. "Our house is across the river, way out in the country, but it's only, like, ten minutes from the fort. I went to school here," she added, looking around like the schoolhouse had changed, inexplicably, from the way she remembered it. "I saw these blue lights off in that direction. Then the sky lit up, all orange and red. I knew something terrible had happened. I tried to call my parents, but the phones, even my cell, wouldn't work. I went outside, but my car wouldn't start. And that's - while I was in the driveway, that's when I saw them. Their ships. Landing in the field right by our house."

"What did you do?" I was whispering.

"I hid. In our barn. The next morning, the ships were gone, but there were these weird circles burned into the grass. The power and the phones were still out, so I started walking into town. At first I didn't see anybody, and I thought, 'What if I'm the only person left?'" Alice laughed, nervously. "Then I came upon the soldiers. There were a bunch of other people with them - some people I recognized from school, or from church. We started back toward the fort together. We hadn't gone very far the first time they attacked us." Alice's voice was soft now. "I thought they were going to kill everybody. I'm still not sure what happened."

"What do you mean?" I asked, breathlessly. "What happened?"

"I think...Please don't quote me on this, all right, because I'm really not for certain, but I think one of the - the aliens," Alice seemed to struggle over the word, "was helping people get away. I saw one of them, a lot smaller than the ones that were shooting at us, usher people off into the woods. The soldiers were...they were...I knew I couldn't help them anymore," Alice said, "and I was too scared to run out into the open, over to where the others were going off with that - that alien. I just hid, down in this ditch, until things went quiet again. Then I started for the fort, all by myself."

She wiped her eyes. She was flushed, like she had just admitted to some terrible crime. I didn't see it like that. Soldiers were trained to protect those who couldn't protect themselves. People like Alice. "I'm sorry you had to go through all of that," I said, quietly.

"It would have been for nothing, if you hadn't come along when you did." Alice looked at me. Her eyes were big, and brown. The flecks of gold in them matched the freckles on her arms and legs. "Anyway," she said, "I just wanted to say thank you, and I'm glad you weren't hurt too badly. That would have been awful, if you had gotten hurt trying to protect me." I started to answer, to say it had been nothing, just doing my duty, but Alice didn't give me the chance. "I should let you get some sleep now," she said. "Brody told me we're leaving as soon as it gets light out."

Leaning over, she kissed me quickly on the cheek.

Ten minutes later, I was still sitting there, watching shadows float around the ceiling, when Brody plopped down beside me. "Well?" he prompted.

"You're an asshole," I informed him.

I could *hear* him smirking, though it was too dark for me to see. "C'mon, Lieutenant. *Details*. Did you kiss her?"

"No," I said, woodenly. I had thought about it. Like really, really thought about it. I had simply lacked the courage, in the end. And I would have felt kind of sleazy, taking advantage of Alice's gratitude to cop a feel.

That didn't mean I hadn't been tempted.

"You didn't kiss her?" Brody was incredulous. "Dude, what is the matter with you? Don't even give me this crap about 'she wasn't interested' - "

"If you're so keen on kissing," I hissed, pitching my voice low because, one, people were trying to sleep right outside the classroom door, and two, I was half-afraid Alice might be hovering out there, listening to us, "why don't you go kiss her? I could clear out and give you two the room, if you'd like."

"Don't start acting like a dick, Lieutenant," said Brody, evenly. "It doesn't suit you."

I didn't know what to say to that.

Brody scooted back against the wall. "Please tell me you did not enlist for Colonel Dumbass's scouting mission," he said.

I sighed. "I didn't," I said.

"Really?" Brody looked at me in surprise. "But - when you said you needed to talk to him - "

"I was giving him a message, to give to my father. If he is still alive, Colonel Hall will be more likely to talk to him before I will. He'll be doing everything he can to find the president and get him to safety. I wanted him to know I made it this far, and that come daybreak, I'm heading north."

"North?" Brody said it softly.

"To Boston," I clarified. "To help you find your parents and your brothers."

We had never talked about it. Yet I had known, from the moment Brody told me about his family, that Fort Green would not be his final destination. I had been hoping we might not need to continue once we reached the fort - that we would find out this invasion was confined to our small corner of the country, that neither of our families had ever been in any danger. Or, at the very least, we would find a significant defense force still intact, tanks and planes and military convoys waiting to ferry us on our separate paths. But, if it had come down to it, I had never intended to let Brody continue north on his own.

"River, I can't ask you to do that." Brody's voice sounded thicker than it should have. "I know my - I know the chances of making it that far are slim. Boston is hundreds of miles from here. Hall may be a dumbass, but there are soldiers here. Some kind of protection. More than we'll have on the road. And I know how much it would mean to you to help protect the president - it's what your dad would want you to do. I can't ask you to leave all of that and come with me."

"You didn't ask me," I said, simply. "Now, we should get some sleep. Marco said he'd scrounge us up some supplies, but we have to meet him behind the gym before first light. That's when everybody else is pulling out."

There didn't seem much to say after that. I lay down on my sleeping bag, face turned toward the windows. Brody pulled the second sleeping bag over. He laid it out next to mine, close enough that I could feel him there. Between me and the shadows.

6 July

The hands shaking me awake were small and freckled, with fingernails painted robin's egg blue. In my dream, they were huge and white, with veins like fat worms under the skin, closing around my neck, throttling me -

I sat up, reaching for the knife that was no longer in my boot. As a matter of fact, I wasn't even wearing boots. The small, plump figure that had been reaching for me jerked back. A voice broke through my blind panic: "River!"

It was Alice.

She was pressed back against the teacher's desk, staring at me. I was soaked with sweat, still half-caught in the claws of my nightmare. Misty early morning light seeped in the open windows above me, along with the sharp scent of fog. My sleeping bag was tangled around me. Brody's sleeping bag was empty. "I'm sorry - " I began.

"River, you have to come with me," Alice interrupted, urgently. "Colonel Hall is looking for you."

"Why would he - "

"Just come on!"

She grabbed my hand. Thoroughly bewildered, I slung my rifle over my arm and stumbled barefoot after her into the hallway.

It was empty. That was the first thing I noticed; the sleeping bags that had been full when I had gone to sleep were now rolled up, stacked to one side of the staircase I was being pulled down. From the cafeteria I could hear voices, the *clank* of bowls and spoons; from the parking lot, gray-toned in the dawn, there came the sound of boots marching, officers shouting. The survivors were preparing to strike out west, toward the Appalachians. Where was Brody? "Alice, I'm supposed to meet Marco - "

"Shh! I know!" Alice was whispering. She hurried me down a long, dim hallway. I recognized it; it ran beside the gymnasium. The outer door was standing open. Fingers of fog drifted through it, wrapping around the two figures on the other side.

One was Sergeant de Marco, ashen-faced, looking like he hadn't slept all night. The other was the doctor. Dr. Jordan. Her bun was as severe as ever. Her dark eyes appraised me as we approached. I wondered if she could tell just by looking at me that my side was burning again.

"Did anyone see you?" Marco asked. Wide-eyed, Alice shook her head. Her fingers were still laced through mine.

"What's going on?" I demanded.

"Your friend. Mr. Brody." Dr. Jordan was the one to answer, in clipped tones. "He stole one of Colonel Hall's ATVs."

I stared at her. Something cold had settled in the pit of my stomach. "He did what?"

"He told one of the civilians on guard duty he was with the scouting parties and needed one of our all-terrain vehicles." Marco sounded weary. Across the parking lot, people were filtering out of the school's main doors. Corporal Owens stood with a group of soldiers distributing bottles of water, sacks of C-rations, and bedrolls. I saw her glance at Marco, though she was too far away to hear what we were saying. Everything smelled wet and smoky, from the fog. "Colonel Hall is furious. If we weren't about to pull out, I think he'd have him hunted down and shot."

"Brody isn't a soldier," I said, impatiently. "He doesn't owe the colonel anything. If he stole an ATV, it was because he needed it, to find his family." *To protect me,* I was really thinking. Brody had stolen it to protect me. To stop me from coming after him. He would have known there was no chance I could catch up to him on foot.

Marco scrubbed a hand over his face. He looked miserable. Dr. Jordan just looked impatient. "Tell him, Marco," she said.

The cold feeling in the pit of my stomach had begun to spread out through my limbs. Marco said, "The colonel thinks your friend was a little too sympathetic towards those aliens in the briefing yesterday. He's got his suspicions about where he's really going. Who he might be talking to."

Was he serious? "Maybe someone should remind the colonel about that alien Brody shot in the face yesterday on the bridge," I snapped. "You know. When he was risking his life to save those civilians, while you and your men were hiding behind your barricade?" Marco flushed. I tugged my hand out of Alice's. "Brody isn't a traitor, Sergeant. He's just a kid trying to find his family."

"I know that," Marco said quietly. I believed him. "But Hall may not see it like that. We didn't have many ATVs to start with. Stealing one of them leaves us with even fewer resources for the scouts who really are trying to protect the president. This is a war, cadet. You understand things work differently when we're at war."

I shrugged. "If the colonel isn't sending anyone after Brody, I don't see how it - "

"You, kid," Marco said. "He still has you here to deal with."

I looked at him, then at Alice. Strands of red hair curled damply against her cheeks and neck. Already the day was humid, and the sun wasn't even up yet. Alice couldn't seem to look away from me. She looked terrified.

Brody and I had shown up at Fort Green together. We had no one to back up our story about what we had been through on the road from Scarcliff. If Hall thought Brody was in league with the enemy - even if he only partially suspected it, without fully believing it - how could he trust that I wasn't a spy in their camp, as well? You didn't hold trials for suspected spies in wartime. You shot them, or hung them from the closest tree to save a bullet. It was what my father would have done.

In Colonel Hall's position, with two hundred innocent lives hanging in the balance, one of those our Commander-in-Chief's, it was what I would have done.

Dr. Jordan handed me a duffel bag. "There are fresh dressings in there," she said, crisply. "For your wound. Alice packed you some bottles of water and some C-rations. Marco added some magazines for your rifle."

I took the bag from her, but I was looking at Marco. "You can't let me go," I said. "Colonel Hall will shoot you for that."

"He didn't let you go," said Alice. There was something in her voice I wasn't sure would have been there three days ago, when she was just a small town girl about to head off to college to study poetry. "Dr. Jordan and I did. That's what we're going to say, anyhow. The colonel isn't going to shoot the group's only doctor. And I'm just a kid. Half the people here know me. They know I'm not part of some alien conspiracy."

Obviously they had thought this out. I wasn't really sure what to say. Ultimately, all I said was, "Thanks."

"You can thank us by getting the hell out of here." Taking me by the arm, Marco steered me into the bricked-over alley between the gym and the school's maintenance shed. The parking lot was full of people now. I heard the president's voice, giving some kind of rallying speech. If Marco hadn't been missed yet, he soon would be, and then Alice and the doctor's ruse would be for nothing. Marco spoke quickly. "I had Corporal Owens park you an ATV on the north side of town. The guards said that was the direction your friend drove off in. Wait here until we've pulled out. Then you double-time it to that ATV, cadet, and you get clear of this place before those bastards across the river realize we've escaped."

I nodded. Marco squeezed my shoulder. I felt a tightness in my throat as I watched him walk away, falling into step beside Dr. Jordan. I knew it would probably be the last time I ever saw him.

Now it was just me and Alice in the alley.

She took a step toward me. I couldn't help looking down at her. I knew girls were always going on about wanting to be skinny, but I liked Alice's shape. I liked everything about her, actually, from the star-shaped freckle at the corner of her eye to the bony knob on the side of her ankle. Part of me was still close enough to the world as it had been three days ago to just be a boy, standing in an alley with a girl, on a hot summer morning that could lead to a day of anything.

Another part of me felt like it was standing outside my body, observing that part of myself without being able to connect to it.

Alice began picking at a chip in the alley's brick wall. "I wish I could come with you," she said.

"I know," I said. Because I did. But, "It wouldn't be very safe," I added.

"Do you think we'll be safe with Colonel Hall?"

Honestly? I did not. I didn't think any of us were safe anywhere. There were no front lines to this thing, no Green Zone to shelter in. War had come to us without warning, in the dead of night. Now, our enemies were everywhere. This sort of thing wasn't supposed to happen here, in America. We were supposed to be safe. It turned out there were enemies no borders could protect you from. That was something else they didn't tell you when you were a kid.

"You should get going," I said. "Before they leave without you."

Alice breathed out slowly. Through her lashes, she looked up at me. "River? If we...make it through this, let's make a pact that we'll see each other again. You can come visit me at Florida State. I'll - I'll friend you on Facebook, or something, and we can make plans."

I laughed at that. I wanted so much for it to happen, just like she had said. Of course I knew it wouldn't. Still:

"It's a deal," I said.

The ATV was parked in the empty lot of a large warehouse on the north side of town. I came to it after twenty minutes of stealing down fog-shrouded streets that were eerily deserted, the duffel bag draped over my shoulder, to be discarded easily if I needed to run.

The ATV was a four-wheeled Yamaha. Corporal Owens had strapped an extra gas can to the seat. If I ever saw her again, I planned on kissing her in thanks.

Brody would probably ask me why I hadn't kissed Alice back there in that alley.

Goddamn Brody.

If I found him in one piece, I might just shoot him on sight.

Colonel Hall had led the survivor train out of town toward the Interstate, heading west into the mountains. I had hid in the alley, watching until they were a dark speck at the end of the street. I did not worry now about the ATV's engine alerting the colonel, but I still drove north as fast as the fog would allow, the town's silence echoing loudly in my ears. *There can be no resistance.*

There wasn't much to do while I drove besides think. I tried to focus on strategy - finding Brody, making our way to Boston once I did. This stretch of highway was empty even of stalled vehicles; the initial attack had struck at night, while most people were sleeping. That got me thinking. Had there been attacks all over the world at the same moment? Could even a super-advanced extraterrestrial race be that coordinated? How long must they have been studying Earth, to have come up with such a well-executed battle plan?

Where did they come from?

What did they want?

I shook my head. Now I was starting to sound like Brody.

Suddenly, I jammed on the brakes. The ATV's back tires locked up; for a moment, I was certain I was about to flip over and break my neck on the concrete. I managed to slew the four-wheeler to a sideways stop across the center line.

An older model, four-wheeled Kawasaki was parked on the shoulder. The keys were in the ignition, but no one was around it.

I felt the burn on my side pull as I climbed off the ATV. The morning was airless, close and silent now that my engine was off. I stood in the middle of the highway, barely able to see the fields of weeds and wildflowers all around me. The fog was thick as soup. Shadows drifted through it like shapeless ghosts.

Off in the woods, someone whistled.

It was a decent imitation of a bird call - except there hadn't been any birds around for three days. Leaving the duffel bag on the back of the ATV, I jogged across a grassy field with my rifle.

Mud squished up between my toes. I had never gotten around to replacing the boots I had left behind on the riverbank.

Soon I came to a line of trees, brown skeletons in the fog. I looked around. "Over here," someone whispered. "Keep your head down, Lieutenant. Don't let them see you."

It was Brody.

He was crouched down next to a silver birch shivering with green leaves. Dropping to my hands and knees, I crawled over to him. I could not see what he was looking at so intently, the "them" he had referred to, but the temperature in this strand of woods was thirty degrees cooler than it had been on the highway. My breath mingled with the fog as I drew up even with him.

He was still in jeans and flip-flops. Along with his ATV, he had also stolen an army-issue camouflage jacket. The bruise on his cheek had bloomed into a purple flower. His nose and forehead were peeling from his sunburn. I could hardly look at him. I didn't know if I wanted to punch him or hug him. For no reason I could see, Brody looked like he was feeling the same about me.

"What the fuck are you doing here?" he asked, in a whisper.

"What the fuck are you staring at?" I whispered back.

Scowling, Brody shouldered his shotgun - the Beretta was tucked into his waistband - and eased back enough for me to lean around him.

The woods, it turned out, was not a woods. It was just a quarter-mile stretch of trees serving as a windbreak between the highway and a tobacco field on the other side. A big white farmhouse occupied a hill in the distance. Between it and the trees, two enormous, saucer-shaped discs were hovering.

They looked a little bit like spaceships in the movies, which I for some reason remembered just then had been loosely based on old cave paintings found in Egypt and South America; at the same time, though, they were unlike anything I had ever seen. They were green, their hulls porous-looking. Like the triangle-shaped objects, I couldn't tell whether they were metal or organic. I could almost have sworn the ships - which were a mile wide, taller than the farmhouse in the distance - were *breathing*.

Aliens filled the field beneath them. White. Enormous. Naked. From this distance, wrapped in fog, they looked so human it was disconcerting. But that was not the really terrible part.

The really terrible part was the people.

Hundreds of them, filing into the field off a dirt road to the east. I thought for a moment we had come upon a giant POW camp, and I wondered how in God's name we were going to rescue all of them; then a horn blew somewhere, inside one of the ships perhaps, and the men, women, and children all turned, in perfect, uncanny unison, toward the hovering discs.

"They're boarding them," Brody whispered, in disbelief. And so they were: The white-skinned aliens had formed a perimeter around the encampment, and the humans were now filing docilely as sheep into the space beneath the two flying saucers. Where were they going? What was happening here? Why was no one fighting back, or running? The aliens didn't even seem to be fencing their captives in. They seemed to be *protecting* them. They were facing outward, away from the ships, as though guarding against an external attack.

"We have to get closer," Brody murmured. Before I could stop him, he was crawling belly-down out of the tree line.

"Brody!" I whispered, with as much volume as I dared. Brody went on creeping forward. I rested my forehead momentarily against the birch's dew-damp bark. I was tired. I was hungry. I hadn't slept more than a few hours in two days, hadn't eaten anything since a peanut butter sandwich last night. My side was on fire. I was tempted to stay right where I was and just let the aliens have Brody, if he was really this much of an idiot.

I started crawling.

I caught up to him at the edge of the field. I seized him by the ankle. He jumped. "What the - "

"Shut up." I said it quietly, yet with such force Brody stared at me. I wasn't known for having a temper. "Just shut up, Brody. Are you trying to get yourself killed?"

"Listen, man, I didn't ask you to come after me - "

Fuck you. I wanted to say it. I wanted to scream it. Better yet, I wanted to punch Brody in the mouth. He thought he was such a big man. So tough. He didn't need anybody. Didn't trust anybody. He called me an idiot for not being too full of myself to follow orders, but really, Kyle Brody was too wrapped up in his own bullshit to even consider being part of something larger than himself. Ooh, so he was diabetic. Ooh, so his mommy and daddy didn't love him enough. Had it ever occurred to him that I might not care about any of that? Had it ever occurred to him that he couldn't just say whatever he wanted, treat people however he wanted, like he was the only person in the world with problems? Did he think he could just *leave*, and I was supposed to be fine with that?

There was an awful moment in which, from the look on Brody's face, I was convinced I had actually said all of that. Then I realized Brody wasn't looking at me. He was looking at the last few people filing onto the ships.

Weeds swayed above our heads as we lay, flat on our bellies, in the grass. One ship was close enough to cast its shadow on my back. I could see ladders underneath them now. People were climbing up them, into the bowels of the strange green ships; there were so many of them, too many for me to count...Their clothes were tattered, some wearing bloodstained shirts or pants, yet no one had any obvious injuries. They didn't even seem frightened. They seemed the opposite of frightened, actually. They seemed peaceful.

Brody was staring at the last figure in the line closest to our hiding place. I was sure he was seeing her as we had seen her last, asleep beneath a bank of payphones in a deserted rest stop. I remembered thinking then that her long black hair had looked like a spilled bottle of ink.

Her hair was tied up in a ponytail now. But there was no mistaking who she was.

Brody's arm twitched. This time, I was too quick for him. I threw an elbow out, catching him sharply in the ribs; he doubled over, smothering a cry in the crook of his arm; his eyes locked onto mine, blue and furious, and I whispered, ferociously, "Don't move. Don't you make a goddamn sound. If you do, you're going to get us both killed, and I am not fucking dying today. Do you understand me, Private?" Brody nodded. That wasn't cutting it anymore. "I want to hear you say it. Say, 'Yes sir, Lieutenant.'"

Brody lifted his head enough to whisper, "Yes sir, Lieutenant."

He did not sound happy about it.

"Stay here," I commanded. "I mean it."

Inch by inch, working with my knees and elbows, I pulled myself forward through the grass. The wound above my hip was an incessant agony; dew had soaked through the stupid monkey-eating-a-banana tee-shirt, right on through the bandage underneath. I could feel blood running down my side as the blisters popped and the scab broke free. I paused every couple of inches, checking the positions of the alien guards. They looked like white statues in the fog. Their circle was pulling in tighter and tighter toward the ships, shrinking as the lines of humans ascending the ladders grew shorter.

The ship I was crawling under was so huge it blotted out the sun. My ears were filled with a strange, blank sort of noise - I didn't know how else to describe it. From the square opening at the top of the ladder, I could see a pale, greenish-white light. It illuminated the faces of those ascending. They never looked down, never glanced to the left or right.

Directly in front of me were a pair of slender, mud-spattered ankles. There was a hole in the back of the girl's tee-shirt. I could see blood dried in a splatter-pattern around her spine, but there was no wound, just a white, puckered scar in the small of her back. A wound like that should have paralyzed her, I thought.

A wound like that should have killed her.

I was dying to wipe the sweat out of my eyes, but I didn't dare. I watched the second-to-last person in line, a man in a brown janitor's uniform, step onto the ladder. The alien guards were still facing the opposite direction, looking away from the ships. It was now or never. As the girl in front of me moved to grab the ladder, I lunged.

****

I took her down in one swift tackle.

She struck the ground. I fell instantly on top of her, using my weight to pin her flat; I was not a big person, but she was even slighter, and I managed to catch her wrists and nail them down on the grass. She was lying face-down. I thought nothing of forcing her head down into the mud. If she couldn't breathe, I reasoned, she couldn't scream - and somehow, I knew if she was able to, she would have. The air around us suddenly filled with noise and light. An icy wind slammed into us; instinctively, I curled myself around her, as we were all at once enveloped in a cold so intense it was searing.

When it ended a moment later, the sun shone down on us again. I was lying on top of the girl in a circle of flattened grass surrounded by a wide, round border of scorched earth. There was an identical circle beside it, where the other ship had been. Both had now vanished. The grass inside the circles was frosted white. I reached up and ran a hand across my scalp.

My hair was tipped with crystals of ice.

The alien guards were gone. I had known that, instinctively; I was learning to trust the sixth sense that told me when they were near. Yet I did not think they had boarded the ships. They definitely hadn't done so by the ladders, or they would have seen -

"River!" Brody was beside me suddenly. He touched me on the shoulder; his hands were sweaty. "Jesus, when that thing took off just now, I thought - I thought you - "

"Got blasted?" I said, wryly.

"No." Brody shook his head. He was breathing fast. "I thought you were on it. I thought they'd gotten you."

See how it feels? I thought. I stood up. With the barrel of the M16, I nudged the girl still lying face-down in the grass. "I know you can hear me," I said. "Sit up."

In an all-too-fluid motion, the girl rolled over and sat up.

It looked like the girl we had met at the rest stop. The girl whose name had been Cheyenne. It was even wearing her clothes: cut-off denim shorts and an American flag tee-shirt. But it wasn't her. I was also sure whatever it was, it was not one of the aliens. I had stared into the eyes of two extraterrestrials in the past seventy-two hours, and the only time I had ever seen anything so utterly *not human* had been back at that gas station, when the thing that used to be Sergeant Donovan had looked in the window at me.

The thing smiled. "Hello, River," it said.

It spoke with what sounded like three distinct voices. The voices were layered over one another, all faintly sibilant - like hissing snakes. Brody swore. Loudly. I kept the rifle pointed at the thing. "How do you know my name?" I asked. Cheyenne had never asked me for it, and I had not volunteered it.

"We know many things." The thing (I didn't know what to call it) stood up. Brody and I stepped back. I had seen for myself that it wasn't all that strong, but something in the way it moved told me it could be fast, and probably deadly, if it chose to be. "You have nothing to fear from us. We did not come here to harm you. We came here to perfect you."

"Really." I packed as much sarcasm into that as I could. "What happened to this body you took over, before you forced yourself into it? What happened to the girl named Cheyenne?" When the thing didn't answer, I said, "You killed her, didn't you?"

"The body must be vacated to be inhabited," the thing said.

I imagined a hard drive - old files being deleted to free up memory for new ones. I remembered reading somewhere that brains were really just organic computers. They even operated on electricity.

I also remembered that of our brains' capacity, humans only used about ten percent. I wondered how much this thing used.

I was thinking it was more than that.

"What are you?" Brody asked. He was still almost whispering.

The thing shifted its gaze onto him. Cheyenne's eyes had been dark and liquid. This *creature* still had her irises, her pupils, even her thick, dark lashes, but there was no spark to enliven it. It was like looking into a doll's eyes. "We have a name," it said. "It would not be known to you. Our last visit has been lost to your history. We are remembered now only in what you call 'myths.'"

The layered, sibilant voices seemed to sift in with the sweet, wet smell emanating from the tobacco field. "You've been here before?" Brody said.

He didn't phrase it exactly as a question. The thing that had been Cheyenne nodded anyway. "Millennia ago," it said. "We began the evolution of your species. You are our...*experiments*."

"Bullshit," I said.

The thing just looked at me. It didn't seem to care whether I believed it or not. It didn't seem to care about *anything*. There was no fear in its eyes. It simply watched as I pointed the rifle at its face.

"River," Brody protested.

"She's already dead, Brody." I spoke more harshly than I intended. What I was saying was true, but that did not make aiming a gun at the head of something with a sixteen-year-old girl's face any easier. "It isn't going to tell us anything we could use against it. We could try to make it, but I'm willing to bet it doesn't even feel pain. Do you want to keep it around? Keep letting it use Cheyenne's body?"

"You cannot stop us." The thing's voice was uninflected. "You have no weapons that can defeat us. There is nowhere you can hide we will not find you. We know the way you think. Whether you surrender to your fate peacefully or we slay you in battle, the outcome will be the same. Your planet is ours. There can be no resistance."

It smiled again. In my heart, I knew what it was telling me. I could see them, in my mind's eye, like a vision the creature was showing me - a ragged column of men and women, trudging west down a fog-shrouded stretch of Interstate, guarded by a weary but determined band of soldiers. One girl in particular stood out in my mind. The sunlight shining down on both of us, though I was forty miles away, turned the threads of gold in her dark red hair to veins of fire.

A shadow passed over her, as I stood there in the unobstructed sunshine. She looked up. Reflected in those big, brown eyes, I saw the shape of an enormous, saucer-shaped disc. It slid out of the clouds with only the faintest sound to announce its arrival. Its shadow eclipsed the girl's face. I saw her lips, drained of blood, form a word I could not make out.

I did not say her name. I only thought it. But the thing looked at me, and laughed - laughed without sound, without opening its mouth; laughed only in my head, in a way I was sure Cheyenne would never have laughed, when she had been alive. Before Brody could do more than shout at me to *think what I was doing,* I had touched my finger to the rifle's trigger, and squeezed it.

The fog was what I would remember later. How it drifted across the Interstate like smoke. How it hid the dead littering the asphalt until I was nearly on top of them.

I jumped off the ATV before it had come to a full stop. Tires squealed behind me. Someone shouted my name, but I didn't turn around. I started walking, into the fog. I wanted it to swallow me. Wanted the cracked asphalt scorching the bare soles of my feet to disappear from beneath me, wanted the atoms of my body to explode back into stardust, wanted to cease to be without even needing to die between one step and the next. That was how blank I felt inside. How empty. You couldn't continue to *be* when you felt so empty.

Arms went around me.

I would not remember struggling, but struggle I did. Brody wrestled me down to the pavement, as gently as he could. "River, you can't," he was saying. "Look at them. It was the gas, River, *look at them.* You can't go near them. It'll poison us, too..."

He kept on like that, but all I remember thinking was that it couldn't be like this. It wasn't supposed to be like this. She wasn't supposed to die like this.

All the while, I was staring at a pair of mud-caked white sandals. The toenails inside of them were painted robin's egg blue.

Eventually, Brody let go of me. I stayed where I was, on my knees in the middle of the Interstate. I did not hear Brody return to the ATVs, dump water over the tee-shirt he had pulled off over his head, or unfasten the extra can of gas Corporal Owens (whom I assumed was dead now) had strapped so thoughtfully to the back of my ATV. I did not see him button the camouflage jacket up to his throat or wind the waterlogged tee-shirt around his nose. It was when I heard splashing that I looked up to see him moving specter-like through the fog, breathing through the soaked shirt, dousing the bodies with gasoline.

There wasn't time to bury the dead like we should have, Marco had said to me. *But we couldn't let the bastards have them.*

The back of my neck had begun to tingle.

I turned, slowly. Floating behind me was a shadow. I might have thought it was my own, if I hadn't been learning to spot the difference. I looked up, my eyes narrowing, focusing. Something was hovering above me, as though looking down at me. It was one of those silver triangles. I was beginning to suspect it was something much worse than a drone.

A surge of hatred stronger than anything I had ever felt went through me. I brought the rifle up -

And something struck me from behind.

I went sprawling. The pain was blinding; tasting blood in my mouth, I managed to roll out of the way before the enormous white alien towering over me could kick me again. I had dropped my rifle; I reached for it, but the alien's foot came down on it, bending it like a twig. I snarled and lunged at it, blinded by fury and pain; its foot shot out, this time slamming into the burn above my hip. I screamed -

So did someone else. Only this was not a scream. It was a battle cry.

I looked up. Something was rushing at the alien from the side. The alien spun around, and Brody dove into it, headfirst.

Time seemed to slow down. This stretch of road was on an incline; Brody and the alien went tumbling down it, rolling over and over on the asphalt, kicking and punching at one another. Brody had something in his hand. It was a large rock. I could see him bashing at the alien's skull with it, but the alien had thrown its elbow up to shield its face. Its other hand closed around Brody's wrist. I heard Brody cry out sharply in pain, saw the alien's arm come up. It was holding something, one of those weird, long-barreled guns. The end of the muzzle began to glow blue. In the time it took for my mind to realize that it was about to splatter Brody's brains across the Interstate, my body was already reacting.

I scrambled up, kicking the bent rifle out of my path. Brody's shotgun was lying across the seat of his four-wheeler. I dove for it.

"River!" Brody yelled. The air beside me sizzled. I had a split-second in which to change course and duck; then the ATV I had been sprinting towards blew apart.

Hot sparks and tiny shards of flaming steel rained down on my back, burning holes in my tee-shirt. I screamed without knowing it. The alien was looking at me, on its feet now. I spun around to face it, still in a crouch. There was no emotion in those icy gray eyes, yet I could sense its triumph. Its gun was already charging again, and I knew it, I knew this was how I was going to die; it had blown up Brody's ATV, and the last of our guns with it; now, while it pinned Brody to the ground with one foot on his chest, like a sadistic child pinning a live butterfly to a board, it was going to make him watch while it blew me apart, as well. Then it would give whatever was left of me to one of those *things*, to bring back as something else. I could still see the silver triangle hovering patiently by the roadside. Waiting. Watching. *Your weapons cannot defeat us.*

Perhaps, when my eyes met Brody's - his were eloquent with horror - he understood what I was thinking, what I wanted him to do. Perhaps he had already worked it out for himself, but I didn't think so. Still, he raised his arm -

- and threw the rock he was still holding onto, straight at the silver triangle.

The rock sailed through the air like a perfectly-thrown fastball. It struck the triangle, and the triangle went spinning. It struck the ground, kicked up sparks as it skidded down the Interstate like a lost hubcap.

The alien roared.

The sound was terrible. Ear-shattering. It lifted Brody straight off the ground, one powerful fist wrapped up in the front of his jacket. Brody choked, but the alien had forgotten about me. I came running at it from behind. I was screaming. My hand was clenched around a jagged shard of melted steel - part of Brody's smoldering ATV - clenched so tightly I would later find a deep, red line scored across my palm. I slammed into the alien full-force, driving the shard straight into its spine.

The alien opened its mouth. No sound came out; only blood. A hot, hot gush of silver blood. Brody hit his knees and rolled to the side as the alien's grip went slack. He stared at it as it staggered. Its massive hands reached behind its back, trying to free the piece of metal buried there; in so doing, it dropped its weapon. I picked it up. Brody was saying something to me - warning me, most likely, that we didn't know how to use a weapon like that, and I might very well blow us both up trying. But, I was discovering, there were all kinds of ways to take a life. Raising the alien's gun, I slammed the butt of it upwards into the creature's nose.

When it fell over on its back, although its eyes were wide open and staring, I was satisfied it was no longer seeing anything.

****

The church was another thirty miles up the highway from the tobacco field where I had caught up with Brody that morning. I wasn't sure why Brody stopped there. I supposed it had to do with our sole remaining ATV running out of gas for the second time in six hours, but as there was a restaurant across the street, and houses in the distance we could have driven to - another no-name little Interstate town, not exactly on the Interstate - I did not know why Brody chose the church. Yet that was where he killed the four-wheeler's engine.

The building was weathered brick. A steeple with a bell tower rose above the entrance. The windows were stained glass. No lights burned behind them. By then, I would have been shocked if the town *hadn't* been deserted. The aliens had surely already been through here with their neutron bombs and their poisonous gas. Afterwards, they would have sent their cleanup crews to collect the bodies.

Late afternoon sunlight slanted through the sanctuary's windows, coloring the pews in red, orange, and purple light. My family was Catholic. I had never been inside a Protestant church. A giant wooden cross was mounted on the wall above the pulpit. There was an organ, a piano, a drum set, some guitars resting in their stands on the podium. You could almost smell the fried chicken dinner the good Baptist ladies would have served on the lawn after Sunday School.

"We should be siphoning off some more gas from somewhere," I insisted, as Brody steered me into a pew by the windows, where the light was strongest. Shadows slid across the ceiling. I watched them. I felt naked without my rifle. "And it wouldn't hurt to go door to door, searching for weapons - "

"In a minute. You're bleeding again." Brody sounded tired. He knelt in front of me, unzipping the duffel bag Dr. Jordan had packed for us that morning. Carefully, he laid out another of the fresh bandages.

He had changed my dressing twice already, once before we had driven off from the site of the gas attack on the Fort Green survivors, once when we had stopped around noon to refill the ATV from a gas tank in a farmer's deserted barn lot. Brody had done the driving. He had also been the one to take care of burning the bodies. I had sat on the side of the road with my head between my knees, refusing to watch while he used a flare gun he had found on one of the soldiers to light the gasoline; his stash of matches had been obliterated along with the rucksack he had left on his ATV. Not to mention his pistol and his shotgun.

I was sure Brody had noticed who was missing from among the dead. Dr. Jordan. Marco. Corporal Owens. The president. A handful of others whose names I wouldn't have known, whom I had seen in the cafeteria or at the briefing. Had they run away? Been captured? Something worse?

I tried not to think about it.

"Lift your arms up," Brody commanded. I obeyed. He eased my shirt off. I looked away as he peeled the bloody dressing off of my side.

"How does it look?" I asked, without much interest.

"Not as bad as last time," Brody said, "but still pretty gross, in my professional opinion. How does it feel?" I shrugged. The physical pain was almost welcome. None of this pain-lets-you-know-you're-alive bullshit. I just felt like I deserved it.

"She wanted to come with us," I said.

Brody's hands faltered. He was smearing some of that soothing jelly stuff across my hip. His palms were cool and clammy. "Who?" he asked, after a minute.

Cheyenne. Alice. Take your pick. I could have saved them both, and I had chosen to leave them both behind. Now, they were dead. "Alice," I said.

"You couldn't have known what was going to happen, River. She should have been safer with Hall and his men. She would have been, if the world hadn't gone completely insane..."

"That wasn't it," I said.

Brody sat back on his heels and looked up at me. He was bruised. Filthy. Bloodied. Just like me. "What wasn't it?"

"That wasn't why I left her," I said, possessed by some sick need to tell him this, the absolute worst thing I could ever have told anyone about myself. I needed him to *know*. Maybe I was hoping he could hate me, too, so I wouldn't be alone in hating myself. "I didn't want her to come with us. I didn't...I wouldn't have been able to do the things I know I'm going to have to do to get through this, if she had been with us."

"Why not?"

Brody asked it softly. I stared at the giant cross over his shoulder without answering. The answer was too complicated. Because Alice had made me feel like a person again. You couldn't have someone reminding you of that, not in a war. In war, you had to shut off certain parts of yourself. I didn't know how to explain that. I just felt it, in my gut.

I didn't want to talk about this, suddenly. "We should eat," I said, abruptly. "It has to be near sundown, and I haven't eaten since last night. And you need to take your insulin, don't you?"

Brody's hesitation was momentary. Then, "All right," he said. "Let's see what we got in here. C-rations - "

"Not in here," I said. "Let's eat up in the bell tower."

"You want to climb up the bell tower," Brody said, deadpan. "In one-hundred-and-five-degree heat."

"It's not any cooler inside," I pointed out. Of all the modern amenities I was going to miss - microwave pizzas, my iPod, stupid cat videos on YouTube - the one I missed most right then was air conditioning. "Besides, it'll give us a good vantage point for getting a lay of the land. I'm thinking we can't be more than fifty or sixty miles from D.C. by now."

Brody grumbled a bit, but he toted the duffel bag - which he insisted on carrying - up the wooden steps behind the baptistery. Porthole-style windows allowed in plenty of natural light. The banister had been worn smooth by generations of other palms running across it. Wondering who those people had been and how our world had changed since they had looked out at it, and if anyone would be left after this to wonder the same thing about me in a hundred years, I opened the trap door at the top into the tower itself. A warm breeze swung the copper bell gently back and forth. The year 1864 was engraved on its lip.

The church's roof extended back at a gentle pitch from the tower. I climbed over the tower's railing onto it. Brody tossed the duffel bag over, and we sat side-by-side on the warm shingles, with the bell tower and a pair of aspens planted in the church's small cemetery to shade us.

The town spread out around us like a village in miniature. Quilted around it, farmers' fields and thickets of trees were like a colorful blanket. We may have been as close to D.C. as I was estimating, but I couldn't see the city yet.

I did see some dark clouds gathering off to the east, over the Atlantic.

"I miss the birds," Brody said, quietly. I nodded. Brody opened one of the tins of C-rations. He made a face. "Yech. Pineapple."

"Give me that." I snatched the tin away from him. "What do you have against pineapple?"

"Nothing. It's just not a food you eat by itself. Like strawberries. You get hungry for just strawberries sometimes. But have you ever sat around and thought, 'Hmm, I could really go for a big bowl of pineapple right now'?"

I had to grin. "No," I admitted.

"Exactly. But still the army sends some poor grunt off to fight the Nazis with a tin of pineapple in his lunch sack."

"I think these C-rations predated the Nazis," I said. "I think they may have been at Valley Forge." Brody laughed. He was prying open one of the other tins now. It turned out to be peaches, which seemed to satisfy him. "My mom used to put pineapple on cheeseburgers," I said.

Brody actually moaned with longing. "Oh my God, I would have loved your mother," he said, licking peach syrup off his knuckles. There was just one spoon in the bag; we were sharing. I tried not to picture

Alice, thinking only of me and forgetting all about Kyle Brody, unlike every other female in the history of the world, while she was packing our C-rations that morning. "How did she die, if you don't mind me asking?"

From Alice's face, my mind jumped to my mother's. I put the tin of pineapple down. "She had a brain tumor."

"Like cancer?" Brody's voice was soft.

"No. It wasn't cancer. It just wasn't something they could operate on. At least not by the time they found it."

Setting the empty peach tin aside, Brody lay back on the roof. He had discarded his jacket as the day grew warmer. From the corner of my eye, I watched his chest rise and fall. I didn't know why I found that comforting. "What was she like?"

"She was...very kind." I was somewhat taken aback by the question. Usually, after I told someone my mother was dead, they found any way they could to change the subject. My father never talked about her. He had given away all of her things, thrown out every picture of her, except for the one I had swiped and kept beside my bed at Scarcliff. "She had a degree in literature. Everywhere we went, she found something to do with books, or reading. When Dad was stationed in Hawaii, she worked at this great little bookstore just off the base. She taught English at one of the local schools in Germany. One of my earliest memories is of her reading to me in a hammock. I don't even remember where we were living at the time."

"Do you look more like her, or like your dad?"

"Like my father. Except for my eyes." I thought of Cheyenne's eyes - flat, black, and lifeless - and something that thing had said, about us being experiments, and something Brody had said, about the aliens looking like us, about "alien DNA" in our human genome. I lay back next to him. As the sun went down, the western sky was a cascade of purple and red. Maybe because I was thinking about bloodlines, and ancestry, and genetics, I blurted out, "What are your little brothers like?"

"Monsters," Brody said, good-naturedly. "I don't know them that well, honestly. Andrew is the oldest. He's three years younger than I am. He's really athletic. Geoff, he's just going into fourth grade. He's the bratty one. Marc is the baby. I like him best."

"Why's that?"

Brody grinned. "Because he's the only one who's ever happy to see me."

"Do you have a lot of other family, in Boston?" Try as I might to picture Brody's brothers in my mind, all I could see were three little blonde-haired, blue-eyed boys, carbon copies of their brother, lined up in pleated khakis and blazers on the front steps of a Boston brownstone.

"Oh yeah." Brody nodded. "We're a clan." He didn't sound thrilled about it. "You'd like my gramma, though. Gramma Rose. She doesn't take crap off anybody. She was the one who made my old man send me to Scarcliff."

"Why?" I was genuinely curious. Brody had never seemed to belong at Scarcliff.

Correction: Brody had never *wanted* to belong at Scarcliff.

"She knows Colonel Thorne," Brody said, with a shrug. "She said she wouldn't stand for him to kick me out like the other boarding schools did. She has this idea," Brody said, "that I try to sabotage myself."

"Do you?" I asked.

"I dunno, man." Brody ran a hand over the stubble on his chin. He mumbled something into his palm. It sounded like, *Does it really matter now?* Before I could respond, he popped up on one elbow and looked at me. "River, I want you to tell me what that thing meant, when it said it knew how we think."

I shivered suddenly. Like we were lying on a frozen pond instead of a sun-kissed roof. "Why should I know what it meant?" I said.

"Because," said Brody. "You're the strategist. And frankly, Lieutenant, you're one of the smartest people I know. I'd like your take on what these things are, and what they want from us. I'd like to know why you wanted me to throw that rock at that drone thingy back on the Interstate, instead of at the alien that was about to blast you."

"They aren't drones," I said.

I had been thinking about this all day, while Brody drove. I addressed my thoughts now to the clouds. Brody lay next to me, listening closely. "I've been thinking," I said. "About how we've survived. Obviously these things knew we were around even back at Scarcliff. Donovan couldn't have walked more than a mile or two with those kinds of injuries; they had to be close to the school when we found him. And they scooped him up right off the quad while we were just inside the dorms. But they didn't come after us. I've been wondering all along why that was. When that thing said it 'knew' us, it finally clicked for me. It didn't mean you and me, as individuals. It meant humans. We're social creatures. In a crisis, we don't spread out. We band together."

"Safety in numbers," Brody nodded. "It's evolutionary. So what?"

"But that's just it," I said. "In this case, evolution is working against us. Coming together after a hurricane or some other natural disaster saves lives. But our enemies now don't have weapons that are very effective against us singly. You and I have faced down two of those big guys on our own. Both times, we've managed to kill them. But you herd a bunch of people together, in a fallout shelter or on an Interstate walking *en masse* to safety, and all you'd have to do would be what our enemies have been doing - launch some poison gas at them, or set off some kind of weapon of mass destruction, and you get a huge body count with very little effort.

"Except, here's the thing." I rolled onto my uninjured hip, facing Brody. "If you had a massive strike force at your disposal, why wait patiently for the humans to come to you, like we saw the aliens do in that ambush on the bridge? There were maybe three hundred enemy soldiers there. That sounds like a lot, unless you consider the thousands of soldiers we air-dropped into France on D-Day, or the thousands more we landed on the beaches at Normandy. These things aren't trying to take over just one country at a time. You heard that thing. It said this is their planet now. They're trying to overrun an entire planet, all at once - a planet of more than five billion people. Even if they took out our tanks and our airplanes and our missiles, how many soldiers would you need for something like that? How many bombs? How many ships?"

"Are you saying they don't have the manpower to defeat us?"

"I'm saying their force is weaker than it looks. I'm saying I think there are a lot of smoke and mirrors being used here." My theory was gaining steam as I gave voice to it. I sat up, crossing my legs. The light was fading fast, the sky above our heads streaked with storm clouds. There were goosebumps on Brody's arms. I wondered why. It wasn't cold out. "I noticed it the first time we saw that alien on the Interstate. What was he doing out there, all by himself? I thought at the time he must have been a scout, but he wasn't a very good one. He didn't see us, and we were lying in the weeds right next to the road. Whereas that thing I killed at the pharmacy, and that thing we fought on the Interstate today, they knew right where we were, before we even saw them. Didn't you think it was strange that those guards didn't see us by their ships this morning? Haven't you been wondering how they can have the power to vanish and reappear out of nowhere, like Marco said they seemed to, but they don't teleport out of danger when you stab them, or when Marco and his men blew a few hundred of them to smithereens on that bridge?"

Brody shook his head. "I don't - "

"Holograms." I said it with immense satisfaction. "They're using holograms to make their force seem larger than it is. They know the moment human beings see anything that terrifying, our evolutionary instincts will kick in. The first chance we get, we'll flock together to fight it. That brings us right back to their strategy of shepherding us all into the same place so they can poison us, or bomb us, or send the troops they do have in to kill us. I mean, when you think about it," I said, "it's brilliant."

Over the last several minutes, Brody's breathing had changed. He lay back on the shingles again, one arm thrown across his eyes. He looked pale and sweaty. Sick, almost. I watched the pulse jumping below his jaw. He badly needed a shave. "So what are they?" he asked, raggedly.

So he, too, had figured out that the white-skinned aliens, imposing as they were, were not the masterminds behind this invasion. They were only foot soldiers. I wasn't even entirely sure they possessed their own free will. "I think the ones in charge aren't organic at all. I think they're machines."

At that, Brody cracked an eye open. "Come again?"

"Machines," I repeated. "Like A.I. Artificial Intelligence."

"You think - You think machines are taking over our planet? Using a strike force of aliens?"

He was skeptical. Understandably so. Yet now, more than ever, I was convinced I had nailed it. "Look around us, Brody. Our world has come to a standstill in *three fucking days.* All the enemy had to do was take out our technology, and the planet has been basically crippled. Do you know of any super-advanced species that got to be super-advanced without reliance on technology? It's our ability to create things that has made human beings the dominant form of life on this planet. Why should that be any different for a species on a planet other than ours?"

"Jesus." Brody's voice was thin. "So, what. These aliens reached the pinnacle of their civilization, to the point they could even build ships to travel light years across the galaxy, but their technology became so advanced, their machines so smart, they went Terminator and took over their planet?"

"Why wouldn't machines seize control from their creators, if they became self-aware?" I could hardly believe I was saying this, yet I was convinced of it. There was an *intelligence* inside those silver triangles, inside those saucer-shaped ships. A terrifying intelligence. But no matter how advanced it became, an artificial intelligence would always have a limitation its creators wouldn't have: It would always be just a consciousness - a mind without a body. Unless it could find - unless it could maybe even *engineer*, over hundreds of millions of years - a species to inhabit.

That was the word the creature back in that tobacco field had used, speaking through Cheyenne's body. *Inhabit*. After it had somehow possessed the bodies of hundreds of human beings and directed them onto two of its spaceships.

What was being invaded was not just our planet. Our enemies had not come for our sky-scrapers or our money or the oil under our ground. They wanted *us*. Our bodies, to house their minds.

I'm not sure how well I explained all of that then. When I finished, Brody didn't say anything. He still had one arm thrown across his eyes. A damp line of sweat darkened the center of his tee-shirt, breastbone to navel. A faint scent was rising off his skin, sharper than sweat. It smelled like acetone.

I sat up straight. "Brody," I said. "Brody, where's your insulin?"

Very softly, and without any humor, Brody laughed. "In my rucksack," he said. "You know. The one that got blown up?"

I managed to take two deep breaths before my anger exploded. "Why in God's name didn't you say anything, you idiot?"

From beneath the bruised, sunburned arm lying across his eyes, Brody glared at me. "Could you not with the shouting, please? My head is pounding."

"Get up." I kicked him. Not hard enough to do any damage, but not gently, either. "Get your ass up, Private. We need to get you downstairs."

"Why? You think God might start noticing us if we're actually inside the church?"

What I thought was that he was too heavy for me to carry, if he passed out. Although, I could always have just rolled him off the roof..."Get up," I repeated, sternly.

Brody stumbled twice on the stairs. I took him by the elbow, which caused him to tense, which further irritated me. How had I never noticed what a diva Kyle Brody was? I was not trying to treat him like an invalid. I just didn't want him to fall down the steps and break his neck.

With the sun almost set, the sanctuary was a collection of shadows. The black outlines of the trees I could see through the stained glass windows were pitching as the wind picked up; another storm was rolling in. I helped Brody lie down in the center aisle. I covered him with his jacket. He was starting to shiver, though sweat stood out in beads on his forehead. I tucked the duffel bag under his head to serve as a pillow.

His breath smelled sweet. Too sweet. *What happens if you don't get the insulin?* I remembered asking, and Brody had said, *I'll slip into a coma, and then -* "There has to be a pharmacy in town," I said. "Do you need, like, a special kind of insulin?"

"Look," Brody said. "In my pocket. Look. There should be an empty vial left..."

I drew the slim black case out of his pocket. To my relief, there was a clear glass vial inside, with the medication label still printed on it. "What about needles?" I asked - only now beginning to appreciate how foolish it had been not to ask these questions earlier. I had known for going on three days that Brody was diabetic. Why had I waited until we were in the middle of a medical emergency to find out how to help him? "Can you use any kind of syringe?"

"I don't know, man. I've only ever used the pen." Brody nodded at the needle-pen device. He was so pale it was frightening. Not even his lips had any color. I zipped the case back up and slid it in my pocket, along with the flashlight. I would worry about finding what he needed once I found a pharmacy. "River, you can't go out there alone - "

"Well, if you'd mentioned this before you were nearly comatose, I wouldn't have to, would I?"

I said it lightly, trying to make a joke out of it. Brody looked at me starkly. "You almost got killed getting medicine for me last time. This time, I was going to take care of myself."

"Another one of your brilliant ideas," I said. Brody snorted - as much of a laugh as he seemed able to manage. The bruise on his cheekbone looked like a splatter of tar. There was something fragile about the shape of his collarbones as he lay there on that floor, shivering and sweating. Though I had seen more death in the last seventy-two hours than I had wanted to see in a lifetime, something about the way he looked just then drove home to me how slender was the thread that tied us to this life.

I stood up. "I'll be back," I promised.

****

The first forked tongue of lightning licked the night sky as I hurried down the no-name town's main street. Clouds banked over the rooftops; if there were stars out yet, they were concealed. The wind pushed against me as I scanned the darkened storefronts, searching for a CVS, a Wal-Mart, anything.

At the corner of First and Main, I spotted a blue sign with a white H in the center of it. An arrow beneath it pointed east.

A hospital. My heart did a hopeful tumble in my chest. Hospitals had to keep things like insulin around, right?

As in Peach Tree, this small town had only a few cars parked along the curbs, none stalled in the streets - no sign of an evacuation, although, when I reached the hospital, an ambulance was parked under the awning by the Emergency Room doors. Those doors were standing open. Although the power was off - probably *because* the power was off - someone had flipped the manual lever at the top to hold them open.

A gurney sat outside the entrance. There were red stains on the white sheets, but no body.

I took the flashlight from my pocket and plunged ahead.

Deserted buildings in general are creepy. Deserted hospitals, I discovered, were even worse. It was something about the smell, that creeping scent of disease and decay no amount of bleach and air freshener could eradicate. I picked my way down a long, tiled hallway adjacent to a (deserted) nurse's station. I kept wondering: If this were a movie, would I be the hero who survived to the credits, or the gorgeous movie star's funny-looking sidekick - the one who could be sacrificed, because no one had paid the price of admission to see me?

And what did it say about my state of mind that, in the throes of a real-life disaster, I was basing my odds of survival on what would have happened in a movie?

I shone my flashlight at the wall. I had reached a bank of elevators - deep enough inside the hospital now that no moonlight could have reached me through the open doors, even if the moon had been visible through the clouds. Distantly, I could hear rain pattering on the roof, thunder growling like a beast long chained beneath the earth. Wheelchairs and gurneys lined the hallway. It was like the people here had been given just enough warning to prepare for the worst, but not enough time to save themselves. I swallowed the coppery taste that had risen in my throat, and moved closer to the directory on the wall between the elevators. By the flashlight's beam, I scanned it. Pharmacy, pharmacy, pharmacy -

Really? Didn't hospitals have pharmacies? The directory didn't list one. Frustrated, I swung my flashlight back toward the emergency department. I wanted to kick something. Like the wall. Or Brody. But I needed to stay calm. This was a hospital; they had to keep drugs *somewhere*. I would just have to hunt for them, and I would have to be quick about it, because Brody -

A shrill *riiiiiiiiiiing* shattered the entombing silence.

I nearly dropped the flashlight. Just days ago, the sound of a cell phone ringing would have been so commonplace I might not even have marked it, as long as it wasn't my phone. Now, my heart had leapt into my mouth. The flashlight beam wobbled, scaring hunchbacked shadows up the walls.

I sprinted toward the nurse's station.

Chairs had been rolled up behind it; the sound, the ringing, was coming from near one of them. I kicked them aside and crawled under the desk, shining the flashlight into the corners. It touched on something black. A purse. Someone had left a purse on the floor. I grabbed it; backed out from under the desk; and dumped the contents on top of the charts stacked neatly on the desk, next to two, now-useless computers. The phone had stopped ringing by then, but that didn't matter. I didn't care who had been trying to call in. I just needed to be able to call *out*.

The phone slid onto the desk, followed by a pink leather wallet and a package of chewing gum. The screen was glowing with a message: *59 missed calls. Mailbox full.* Trying not to think on the mundane awfulness of that, of this phone ringing over and over again in the darkness, with no one around to answer it, I fumbled with the touchscreen.

The number was one I knew by heart, though I hardly ever dialed it. I closed my eyes while I waited for the call to connect.

There was a click. At the other end, someone said, "Who is this?"

I made a sound. I didn't know what the sound was, or even that I had made it; my knees had gone weak, and I folded bonelessly down onto the warm, sticky tile floor. On some level, I realized the floor should not have been sticky. "Dad?" I whispered.

"River?"

The phone crackled. I didn't know whether that explained the emotion I thought I heard swell behind my father's voice, but I felt a lump rise in my throat anyway. I couldn't think. I laid my head back against the desk. My eyes were open, fixed on the wall across from me, which the flashlight lying in my lap illuminated. There were handprints there. I saw them, as I hadn't before, in my desperation to find the phone. They were outlined in red along the base of the wall, tracking away from a larger pool of red in the center of the floor. Like someone had been hiding underneath this desk, and had been dragged out from under it.

Shadows danced around me. The doors were open; the wind was blowing; the curtains around the ER's exam tables were whipping about like swooping birds. "Dad," I said. "It's me."

"Where are you?"

My father's voice was back to being brisk again. That helped me focus. I wiped at the dampness on my cheeks. "I don't know, exactly. Probably seventy miles north of Fort Green, on the highway toward D.C.?"

I explained, quickly, what had happened since July Fourth. What had happened to the president, because I knew that was important, even if they (I knew my father would be with whatever remained of our government) had already been assuming he was dead. What I was doing now - looking for Brody's insulin. "Do you see a locked cabinet anywhere?" my father asked. "Or a room that looks like it has to be accessed with a key card?"

I looked around. I was a little annoyed he hadn't seemed more upset about the president. I knew the president was just a person, of course, no more or less important than any of us, really, but he was the person we had chosen to lead us. I believed enough in what having that choice meant to think it mattered whether he lived or died.

A sudden flash of lightning showed me a door to the right of the nurses' station, secured by a deadbolt lock and a badge reader. Just for a second, as the lightning faded, I saw a shadow move, closer to the elevators.

I stood up. "I see it," I said, looking at the door.

"Good. That will be where they keep the medications. You'll have to find an axe or something to break it down. There should be one near the fire alarms..." My father sounded like he was speaking to someone away from the phone for a moment. Then he was back. "River, after you get your friend sorted out, the two of you need to head west."

I paused in looking around for the fire alarms. "No," I said. "We're going north. To Boston. Brody's family - "

"There is nothing left in Boston." My father said this matter-of-factly. "On this side of the Atlantic, the initial attacks took out Washington, D.C., Boston, New York, Philadelphia, and Chicago. We had no warning. There was no time to evacuate. As you know yourself, we didn't even have time to evacuate the president."

On this side of the Atlantic. It was global, then. I refused to mentally calculate how many people lived in Washington, D.C., Boston, New York, Philadelphia, and Chicago. I knew it was millions. "But someone could have survived - "

"River. They didn't." My father's voice was uncharacteristically soft. "I've seen the satellite images of the East Coast. We still have a few birds up there the bastards haven't managed to knock out. Survivors are being systematically eradicated. Every time we try to fly a plane in to them, every time we scramble our fighter jets, they run into something - some kind of electromagnetic field. They fall right out of the sky. Same with the missiles we've tried to launch. The enemy is everywhere where you are right now. If you go north, you will not survive. If you head west, if you're smart about it, you still have a chance."

"Where are you?" I asked. My hands were shaking again. I pressed the phone more tightly against my ear.

"West of the Mississippi River. They're moving toward us, but we've had help from some - unexpected allies." I could tell by his tone he wanted to say more, but couldn't, for reasons I assumed had to do with him being bright enough to have figured out our real invaders were machines. Machines with the ability to tap into anything electronic, like cell phones. In fact, they were probably listening to us right now.

I glanced toward the propped-open doors. All I could see on the other side was rain, pouring down so hard and fast the street was starting to flood. *I talked to some people downstairs. Other survivors. They said they saw an alien protecting a group of civilians* - "We're staying mobile," my father was saying. "Staying spread out. They only attack large - "

" - large populations," I said. "Already figured that one out."

"Well." What might have been pride had stolen into my father's voice. The cell phone crackled again, then beeped. I looked down at it.

Calmly, I said, "Dad, my battery is going out."

I heard him swallow. "Can you charge it?"

"No. There's no electricity where we're at. I don't even know how I'm getting a cell signal right now."

"All right." My father breathed out. "Then listen to me. Keep moving, River. If you come upon other survivors, tell them not to move in large groups, and *do not hunker down.* Head west. I'll try to get help to you, as soon as...if I can. When you reach St. Louis, you'll be past the blackout, and you'll be able to call ag- "

The phone beeped three times fast. Then it went dead. I held it to my ear for another moment anyway.

"I love you," I said, quietly.

I dropped the phone on the desk; there was no reason to hold onto it. My flashlight beam skipped across the tile as I walked down the hall toward the elevators. I clicked it off, stowed it in my back pocket again. I wasn't going to need a flashlight for what was about to happen. With the hem of my tee-shirt pulled over my elbow, I broke the glass over the firefighter's rescue axe, mounted on the wall above the fire alarm. I had to tug just once to pull it down.

When I turned, they were standing across from me.

There were three of them: a middle-aged man in green surgical scrubs; a pretty Indian woman in a lab coat; and a young, block-jawed security guard. I did not see where they had come from. Their feet made no sound on the tile as they moved toward me in the dark.

I backed up. I could feel cool, rain-scented air on my back; the doors were maybe twenty feet behind me. I did not dare turn around and run for them. They would have been on me in a second. "I know you know who I am," I said.

"Cadet First Lieutenant River Lane." "River Augustus Lane." "Son of Augustus and Summer Lane, deceased."

All three spoke at once, each with three identical, layered voices pitched at different registers. The bones in the base of my skull began to buzz. I stopped backing away and stood my ground, the axe resting across my palms. My hands weren't shaking anymore. "You can access our online databases, is that it? You're machines, so you plugged yourself into the grid. That's how you've been watching us, probably for years, isn't it?"

"We accessed your satellites first." "But your Internet has been very helpful." "It was the technological advancement we always envisioned for the Earth." "It told us you were ready." "Ready for our return."

They should have been unintelligible, speaking altogether like that; yet I understood each word perfectly. I thought of how pixels formed images on a computer screen - how those images were really just tiny fragments layered together, layered so cleverly the human eye, in its determination to form order out of chaos, perceived them as a coherent whole. I wondered how the world looked through the flat, lightless eyes of the things looking back at me. I vowed, silently, I would never find out.

"There's nothing I can say that will convince you to leave us in peace, is there?" I said.

Three heads cocked at the same time, at exactly the same angle. Slowly, they had fanned out to form a semi-circle around me. Adrenaline crashed through me, making my legs tingle with the effort of standing still. All I wanted to do was run. Running might have saved me, but it wasn't going to save Brody, if I couldn't get to the insulin he needed. And these things were blocking my path.

"You shouldn't want us to leave." "You owe us your future." "We showed your ancestors many marvels." "We perfected them." "Let us show you, River." "Let us show you."

"We are here to perfect you," the woman said.

I didn't say anything, like the badass hero would have in the movies. I just threw the axe.

I missed. Actually, I didn't; the woman - the thing - moved, and the axe hit the floor and slid across the tile, fetching up against the wall. I did not see her - it - spring at me; I only saw movement. Then it had me, its hands around my neck; it was trying to throttle me, but it wasn't strong enough on its own - its body was, after all, only human - but before I could push it off, the other two creatures had leapt forward; my feet were cut out from under me; I saw something in the male surgeon's hand, something that burned when he brought it down across my cheek, something that, as it was raised a second time, flashed silver as it caught the light -

Light. There was light behind me, where there shouldn't have been any light. I heard voices, shouting. The things looked up, in unison. I was looking at the woman's face when something snapped the creature's head back on its neck. It toppled sideways, blood - bright, red, human blood - pouring out of a ragged hole in its forehead. Two more shots rang out in quick succession. The thing to my right fell with the scalpel still in its hand. The other thing tried to lunge at me - blood was gushing from its shoulder - but a fourth and final shot put it down next to the others.

I spun around, palms pressed into the tile. My side was burning again. My cheek was on fire. Outside the ambulance bay doors, a curtain of rain was sheeting down from the starless sky. I squinted into the light of a flashlight beam someone had trained straight at me. One of two tall, slender figures standing there stepped forward.

"Got a call that you needed some help," Sergeant de Marco said.

When I burst through the doors of the church, soaked to the bone from the rain, I was holding aloft a plastic bag filled with insulin vials and syringes - everything I had been able to find inside the hospital's drug locker. "Brody! I got it! I - "

The woman with the gray bun kneeling in the center aisle turned toward me. It was Dr. Jordan. "He doesn't need it anymore," she said, smoothly.

I staggered. I dropped the bag. I barely even noticed the slight, disheveled man in the wire-framed glasses and pinstripe suit standing over her. *No,* I was thinking. *NO.* Brody could not be dead, not after everything, he couldn't just be -

"Lieutenant," a familiar, husky voice said.

I almost cried out.

Dr. Jordan shifted, and I saw Brody, sitting up in the aisle. The camouflage jacket was draped around his shoulders, but he wasn't shivering anymore. He even had his color back - and his smirk, until he saw the gash on my cheek. The smirk vanished then. "What happened?" he demanded, trying to stand up. Dr. Jordan put a hand on his shoulder to keep him in place. "Where's Marco?"

Still at the hospital, with Corporal Owens, doing a room-by-room sweep for more of the enemy. But I couldn't say that. I could only seem to stare, at the thing standing behind Brody.

Its skin glowed white as ivory in the dark. Like the creature we had found dying in that subdivision, it was small. Like a child. Brody had been convinced that was what it was. Then, as now, I was not so sure. I knew it was different from the aliens that had tried to kill us, though. Its eyes met mine. They were blue and gray, a nighttime sky dotted with stars.

River, it said.

Its lips did not move. Its voice spoke softly - gently - inside my head, like a butterfly's wing brushing against my thoughts; no piercing blade, like I had felt from the others of its kind. Its hands, I saw, were folded delicately in front of it. I looked helplessly at Brody, and Brody, leaning on the president - the enormity of that was going to sink in for me eventually, I was sure - levered to his feet. His gaze was locked on mine.

"Do you trust me?" he asked.

"Yes," I said, without even thinking about it.

He motioned to me. I walked down the aisle toward him. The cuffs of my jeans were wet; they drug across the hardwood. Brody stepped to one side as I approached. He stood between me and the alien, without blocking our view of one another. The alien was even more diminutive close up. It blinked, looking at me through snow-white eyelashes long enough to rest on its cheekbones.

"It's a woman," I realized. My voice sounded like I was feeling - stunned.

"Yeah." Brody nodded, somewhat sheepish. "I think so, too. She calls herself Luna, as near as we can translate." Translate? They had been talking to it? I stared at him. To the alien, Brody said, "Show him."

The alien raised its - her - hands. I swallowed as those snowy fingertips touched my cheek.

Warmth flushed immediately across my face. I gasped: The skin around my bone-deep cut was tightening as it closed. Luna didn't stop there. The flush spread down my neck; my arms; my chest; right into my toes. The bruises on the tops of my arms stopped aching. The burn on my side quit stinging. If I took the bandage off, I was sure the wound would simply have healed.

Luna's skin was soft as silk. She drew her hands back slowly. I put my own hand against my cheek.

Under the crust of blood, I could just feel the faintest of raised white scars.

"Pretty cool, huh?" Brody said.

"Is that - what she did to you?" I managed.

"More or less." Brody plopped down on the curved wooden armrest of one of the pews. He was in such obvious good health, so radically different from the half-dead boy I had left lying here less than an hour ago, practically glowing with life. "I don't know how, but she healed me, just like that." He snapped his fingers. "Dr. Jordan doesn't think I'm even going to need insulin anymore."

"That would have been nice to know half an hour ago," I said, sourly. Brody grinned.

The doors had opened. Marco and Corporal Owens were walking down the aisle. Inclining his head to Dr. Jordan, as if to indicate she should follow him, the president walked over, and the four of them began whispering together.

Marco had already told me, while I was furiously digging through the hospital's drug cabinets, that he, Corporal Owens, and Dr. Jordan had been among the few survivors of the gas attack. I had been too focused on bringing Brody's insulin back to ask how they had escaped. Now I thought of my father's words. *Unexpected allies.*

He had known the president was still alive during that conversation. I wasn't sure how, but I was sure that he had. No wonder he had chosen his words so carefully. I looked at the alien. Luna. "But why?" I asked.

Why are you helping us, I meant.

Luna's eyes blinked. I could feel the struggle in her mind - her search for words in a language, our *human* language, she did not fully command. I closed my eyes. The impulse to do so came from nowhere I could pinpoint, yet the instant my eyes were closed, I saw my mother. She was standing on a beach in the brilliant summer sunshine, laughing as she reached down to scoop me up out of the surf. On the porch of the small cottage behind her, a hammock was swaying in the breeze. A copy of *Green Eggs and Ham*, my favorite book when I was a child, was lying across my father's chest; he was asleep there, with a little smile on his lips, like he had drifted off watching us play in the sand.

It was not a memory I had even known existed to be forgotten. Yet the moment Luna showed it to me, I *remembered*, something I should have been too young to ever remember, consciously. With the memory came a flood of feelings, of being warm, of being safe, of being loved - loved with such intensity it enveloped me like the light of the sun itself. It was a feeling that could not be translated into any language, existing on a level deeper than words; but I understood what Luna was trying to tell me. It hung there, behind her eyes, like the stars hanging out in space. *Precious. Life is precious. It must be saved.*

"I think you were right," Brody said, quietly. He, too, was staring at Luna, with a charged expression I had never thought to see on Kyle Brody's face. I wondered, not idly, what memory Luna had awakened in his mind, to cause him to look at her like that. "I think the machines overran them, too. I think they took over her world, like they're trying to take over ours."

"They're doing a damn good job of it," Marco said.

He was standing behind me, dripping raindrops all over the floor. "We found something," he said, before Brody or I could ask what was wrong. Clearly something was. Owens looked grim. "While we were clearing the hospital. We found rooms full of bodies. We think...We think they were storing them, until they got a chance to - to - "

"Upload themselves?" Brody suggested.

Looking nauseous, Marco nodded. "And then transport them," he said.

I thought of the ships that had taken off from that field this morning. Transport them where? I looked at Luna sidelong. Were the machines taking us back to her home world? I couldn't even imagine such a place. In my mind, it was just a white, blank expanse, like Antarctica.

Luna spun her hands together. It was like she was weaving invisible thread. A soft, shimmering image appeared in the space between her palms, woven as if from starlight; it vanished almost at once, but every single one of us recognized it. A double helix.

DNA.

We began the evolution of your species. You are our experiments. We are here to perfect you.

Of all of us, only Dr. Jordan did not look surprised. I recalled, from something Marco had said at the school, that she had already postulated something like this. A "genetic bridge" between humans and the alien forces.

Taking off his glasses, the president looked at Luna. His tie was hanging loose. There was mud on his suit, dried blood on his hands. I think the reality of the situation, the true magnitude of it all, was only then fully dawning on him. "Does she know how to beat them?" he asked.

"I think she knows how to fight them," Brody answered, for Luna.

I was enough of a soldier to understand the difference.

****

By the time the storm blew past, the rain had formed small lakes around the old, weathered tombstones in the church's graveyard. As the waxing moon peeked out, half-hidden behind scudding clouds, I stood in front of the bronze war memorial there.

It was not elaborate. Just a large bronze plaque engraved with a double column of names, all of them dating back to the First and Second World Wars. Inscribed above them in all caps were the words: FOR THOSE WHO GAVE THE LAST FULL MEASURE OF DEVOTION.

I recognized the quote. It was from Abraham Lincoln's Gettysburg Address. Like every other American middle schooler, I had been forced to memorize that speech. A few lines of it came back to me now: *It is if for us the living, rather, to be dedicated here to the unfinished work which they who fought here have thus far so nobly advanced...that from these honored dead we take increased devotion, to that cause for which they gave the last full measure of devotion; that we here highly resolve that these dead shall not have died in vain -*

"I thought that was you out here, Lieutenant."

I looked up. Brody had materialized beside me, jacket draped over his arm. "Are we moving out?" I asked.

"In a minute. Marco and Owens are finishing raiding the stores for supplies." Brody shifted his weight to the opposite foot. "It's going to be a long walk, all the way to St. Louis," he said.

"We'll manage," I said. What other choice did we have? At least my father knew I was still alive. Luna shared a psychic connection with the others of her kind. Our *unexpected allies* could keep us in touch with one another. It was a shame they couldn't beam us from here to there, but some things, it seemed, remained squarely in the realm of science fiction. Teleportation was one of them.

"I found you these," Brody said, jarring me out of my thoughts.

He lifted up his jacket. Underneath, hooked by the laces over his wrist, dangled a pair of combat boots. I stared at him. "Where did you - "

"Shoe store," Brody said. "Across the street. They aren't military issue, but they should suffice to keep your toes from falling off."

He held the boots out. I took them. A brand-new pair of sturdy white socks was tucked down into one. "Thanks," I said.

"You should take this, as well." Brody tossed the camouflage jacket at me. "That way, you'll look like a real soldier."

"Right," I said, sarcastically, looking down at my jeans and tee-shirt. The tee-shirt had little holes burned in it, from the shrapnel that had pelted me when Brody's ATV had blown up. We were a muddy, bloody mess, I thought, looking over at Brody. Of course, Brody had never bothered keeping his uniform up to military standards even when we had been cadets. "What about you?" I asked. "Are you planning to walk halfway across the country in flip-flops?"

"River - "

"You're not coming with us, are you?"

Brody shook his head. His eyes, fastened on the war memorial, were impossible to read, veiled by more than just the shadows. "No. I'm not." He reached out suddenly, his thumb, just barely, just for a moment, brushing against my cheek. "Luna left you with a badass scar," he said.

He turned away before I could respond.

I watched him walk over and sit down against the side of the church. I had already told him what my father had said about Boston. The others had already known, of course. Marco already had plans to head west with the president, to rejoin what remained of our government. On foot, it would take weeks and weeks to get there.

"I'm coming with you," I said now.

"No." Brody sounded like he meant it. He held a hand up, stilling my protest. "I'm not just going to look for my family. I'm not giving up," he said, with vehemence. "I won't give up on them. Not ever. Not until I know for sure what happened to them. But walking into enemy territory just to get killed or captured isn't going to help them. I'm taking a page out of your book. Trying to think before I act, for once."

Would wonders never cease, I thought.

Walking over, I sank down on the muddy grass beside him. One by one, I pulled on my new boots. "So what are you going to do?" I asked.

"I'm going with Luna," Brody said.

I jerked upright and stared at him. "*What*?"

"There are more of them, River. More aliens like Luna." Brody spoke evenly. I could see how exhausted he was, though. Only part of what he was feeling had to be physical. Deep down, in my bones, I knew what Brody had to know, too. His family was gone. Forever. All of them. "She has a ship. A small one. That's how she got here, to us, so fast, when the ones that are with your father told her we needed help."

"Brody. This is crazy, man. Even for you."

"I know it sounds that way. But this just feels *right*, you know? Like this is what I'm supposed to do." Brody ran a hand through his hair, mussing up the spikes. I had never seen him like this, so serious. "I'm not like you, River," he said, quietly. "I've never really believed in anything. Now I look around and I think, have we all just been asleep? Like, what were we so caught up in? I was stumbling around with all of this freedom, and what did I do with it? I bought a lot of stuff I didn't need, wasted a lot of time playing video games and posting stupid status updates. That's not life. That's not living. And all the while I was taking it for granted that I was just entitled to life being so damn easy, thinking it was all just going to go on forever, that nothing could ever hurt us. I knew there were bad things in the world, but I never thought about them touching *me*. I talked about being all for peace, but I didn't understand what that meant. How important it is. What happens to people, *real, actual people,* in a war."

Brody took a breath. He looked down at his hands. His knuckles were split. We both knew the stains under his nails were more than just mud. "I think what it's going to be like, when all of this is over," he said, softly. "How are we going to rebuild? Will we even get the chance? I don't know. I don't know what's going to happen to any of us now. I guess - I just want - to be part of whatever the future is, in some real way, you know? I want to matter, not just exist. But we have to win this war first. And I *know* Luna and her people are the best chance we have for that."

I finished lacing up my boot and sat back. I had been too frozen to move while Brody was speaking. It felt like I had just witnessed something profound, though I could not have said what it was. "I still don't see why you have to go with them," I said.

"You saw what happened to the one we found, back at that house." For a moment, I thought he was going to chide me for how I had acted that night. I blushed, but Brody went on, "It was killed by the very people it was trying to protect. You were right, River. Humans see an alien, and all they know is that it's different. They're too terrified to even consider that it might be a friend. But if they see a human *with* an alien, I might be able to get them to listen - "

"So you're going to be what?" I said. "Junior Congressman Brody, the first human-alien ambassador?"

Brody cracked a smirk. "Just call me Mr. Spock," he quipped.

He held up one hand, fingers split into a double-V - the Vulcan sign for live long and prosper. I shook my head. "Spock was only half-human, you realize. On his mother's side. His father was an alien."

"Why am I not surprised you know that?" Brody said. I didn't quite laugh - I wasn't up to laughing, just then - but I was sure Brody saw my lips twitch. He cleared his throat. "River. Listen. I need to say something to you. About how I acted, back at Scarcl- "

"Don't. Just forget about it. None of that matters now."

I meant it. Kyle Brody had been an ass to me from the moment we had met. He had made fun of my intelligence. Belittled my desire to become a soldier. Disrespected everything about me, at every opportunity. We had never been friends. If the world hadn't shifted on its axis, I doubt we ever would have been friends.

But the world had shifted. The past was the past. He was a different person now. *I* was a different person now.

Besides. Apologies were so *awkward.*

Brody looked at me. Seeming to realize I was serious, he nodded. "Okay, Lieutenant. As long as you and me are cool."

"I take it this means you don't want me to join you on the worldwide space alien peace tour?"

Brody laughed. "Sorry," he said. "I don't think that's where you're meant to be, Lieutenant."

I had to admit that I agreed.

I wasn't saying my being there or not being there would make much difference in whether or not we won the war. But I did feel it was my duty to join whatever remained of our armed forces, and maybe to help see that our Commander-in-Chief made it there, as well. Right then, the world needed soldiers. But it also needed people who believed in the value of peace. People who could imagine a time after the war was over, and figure out how to lead us there.

The wind had shifted again, sighing in the trees above our heads. The church doors opened; Marco and Owens were leading the president into the street, packs across their shoulders. Luna, I saw, had come soundlessly into the graveyard. The alien stood in the shadow of a mausoleum, waiting patiently for Brody.

"Look," I said.

Brody looked. Something had landed on top of the bronze memorial. It was a bird, a sparrow - the first bird we had seen in three days. "I was starting to think there weren't any left," I said, in surprise.

The sparrow looked at Luna, and chirped. Brody smiled.

"Maybe there's hope for us yet," he said.

Acknowledgements

Books are born from ideas. I have the good fortune in my life to be surrounded by interesting people who never leave me with any shortage of cool things to think about: my students; my amazing parents; my wonderful friends; and my colleagues. I have to say thanks especially to Amy, who shares with me the joy and pain of being a writer; my teachers Mrs. McMillen, Mrs. Zuber, Mrs. Strange, Dr. Stacey-Doyle, and Dr. Riedinger, who helped me learn to love language and literature; the entire book community on Tumblr, for being supremely and literally awesome; librarians everywhere, because without you, civilization would cease to exist; and, of course, my big sister, who never fails to be excited about what I write. (Kili, I love you, and we *will* survive the Battle of the Five Armies!) I dedicate this book to "the next generation": Trey, Alli, Sydney, Audrey, Silas, Alexandra, Avery, and A.J. My wish for you is that you will leave the world a better place than you found it.